The Billionaire's Nanny

S.E. Riley

The Redherring Publishing House

The Billionaire's Nanny

Table of Contents

Chapter 1

Sophie

The plane dipped low, under the cloud bank, and from the cockpit window, I saw it. It had been fourteen years since I'd left Criker's Isle, but nothing could have prepared me for the sight of that beautiful, terrible place.

Crags and cliffs rose to the island's North and South, their black heights a stalwart defense against the roiling turmoil of the Atlantic. High on the island's southern side, I could already see the farmland and fields where I'd played as a child. These sat at the base of a high stretch of hills that rose to a dizzying peak nestled in a thick blanket of dark pines. Beyond Mount Criker, barely visible through the mist were miles of grassland and a forest that wrapped thick, dark arms around the eastern plateau.

To the West, though, at the base of the foothills, lay a tiny, dark spot amongst the murky green of the island, a ramshackle polka-pattern of villages, houses, and winding gray roads which latticed a forlorn opening to the sea. There, by the water, lay Fairtown. The place I'd grown up. The site of all my fears. I almost laughed to think this brazen outpost of human life, the last and

1

westernmost outpost of human hopes and ambitions, was hardly visible from up here in the sky.

We began our final descent, buffeted by sea winds whose blows rocked the wings of the tiny Cessna I'd chartered for my prodigal return. The ferry was out that day; a bad storm had blown its motor, and I'd had to fly instead. I clutched my bag tighter as we plunged through the rain and the fog until the lights of an airstrip nestled in a small valley started to glow through the mist.

We landed bumpily but safely, and as the plane skittered to a slow halt, I felt the knot in my stomach start to unwind. It was already growing dark. September had cast leaves from trees and drawn ugly streaks of water and mud across the airfield. The pilot sighed and turned to me.

"That's where he'll be. In the shack, over there," he said gruffly.

He pointed to a shining light in the distance, and as I peered through the rainfall, a cabin disclosed its shape. I undid the latch on the door, taken aback by the thin layer of metal that had sat between me and the four thousand feet we'd summitted to on our journey. I thanked the pilot and descended, hefting my heavy bag towards the shack, my heart beating with nerves.

The last time my father and I had locked eyes with one another had been the day I left. Echoes of screaming and crying passed through my mind as I recalled that day. There had been no letters, no calls, no contact of any kind between us in all that time. The last time I'd seen him, he'd been the one flying the planes. The pilot, a nice kid from town called Jake, had told me arthritis and old age had made the daily flight too much for my father. That made me worried about the state of the man whose life I was about to crash into.

As I approached the shack, to my surprise, the door opened. And twenty feet from the porch of the old wooden hutch where I had stopped stood my dad, framed by the doorway to his sides and the bank of radios and transmitters behind him. Craig Gardner. For a moment, we said nothing; each struck still by the suddenness of the meeting.

"Hello, Sophie," he said with a tired smile. "It's been a long time."

"Hey, dad," I said. "How's mom?"

His face clouded over. "Fine," he said. "Just fine."

A silence grew between us, the roar of the rain and the wind deafened by the weight of years and memories.

"I need to get back to work, Sophie," he said. "But I'll see you, I guess."

I let a mirthless laugh escape my lips and turned away as he retreated into his office and shut the door.

Same old dad. Rather ignore me than cross mom.

It had always been that way. No idea why I had thought it would be any different after all these years.

Sighing, I grabbed my bag and crossed the field as the rain soaked me to the bone. My fingers trembled as I undid the latch on the wooden gate, which opened onto the hiker's trail into town. It led down the hill towards Fairtown, and as I looked through the treeline, I could already glimpse the gray, terrible waves battering and soaking the jetty. My shoes were already stained with mud.

It was a short walk down the road leading into town. I looked across the fields and slopes, casting their long, high shadows on the town. Even now, it still looked the same as when I'd left, even after regeneration and tourism had come to the island. Another sad, small whaling town abandoned by the mainland. No wonder I'd taken any chance to leave this place when I was younger, no matter how dangerous or how much my escape had changed my life forever.

As I struggled through the rain, the strap of my heavy bag digging through my shoulders, I heard the blip of a police siren behind me and a car engine growl through the rain as it pulled onto the side of the road.

"Sophie! Hey, Sophie!"

I turned around to see a young man hop out of the open door of his car. My youngest brother, Trevor. Years had filled out Trevor's face, and a golden, well-trimmed beard lay on his cheeks where once they'd been soft and bare, but I could recognize him even in his police uniform as the wind threw up a gust, and the rains whipped my cheeks.

"As I live and breathe," I said, taking him in.

"Come out of this rain, will ya? Let me give you a ride?" he said.

I stumbled towards him, almost slipping on the wet tarmac, and opened my arms, dropping my bag. He hugged me gently.

"Been too long, sis," he said as I sheepishly picked up my belongings and slung myself into the passenger seat of the police car. As we sat next to each other, laughing a little and wiping the rain from our faces and hair, I saw *DEPUTY SHERIFF* written on the back of his brown jacket in bold yellow letters.

"How did you know I'd be here?" I said. I'd mentioned nothing of my arrival to my family. I'd never tried to contact them, not since the night Trevor freed me from my awful life with his meager savings, and I started to run, run, and had never stopped running from my past.

"They told me someone with your name was booked on the plane. You can imagine how quickly news spread around here that you were coming back. Fairtown's prodigal daughter returns." He shook his head, stroking his beard. "I couldn't believe it when I read the passenger log, so I drove straight up here to meet you. Dad doesn't know. I know. I don't think Mom or Bee even know you're here yet."

I sighed, and the past soured the happiness of our reunion. "I was going to let you know, somehow. But it's been so long, Trevor. I wouldn't even know how to get in touch with you guys now."

Trevor started the car, and we began to drive down the road into town. "I'm so glad you're back, Sophie. I missed you. I really did."

As the worn-out roads and creaky old buildings of Fairtown passed into view, I was submerged in memories. "I never got the chance to thank you properly, Trevor," I said. "I owe it all to you."

It was true. When I was sixteen, I'd left Criker's Isle for the last time, wanting a better life, with reckless, teenage love beckoning me to the mainland. Derrick, my boyfriend, the guy I ran away with, was everything my parents didn't want for me. Protective and strong, Derrick had been a teenage runaway, just one year older than me. He was an angry young man with a penchant for taking chances. We'd been madly in love, and suffocated by the coldness and distance I'd grown up with, I'd escaped for the sake of a better life, a life not imprisoned on Criker's Isle. My mom, Alice, and my older sister, Belinda, had cut me off straight away.

As Derrick and I squandered my savings on cheap, run-down apartments and hopeless dreams, only my dad and Trevor had kept contact with me. And when Derrick changed, I realized that Trevor was the only person I had in the world.

Protective, strong. Did I say that? Controlling, a bully. Those were the words I'd meant to say. In the final months of our time together, all of the tenderness I'd come to know from Derrick drained right out of him and replaced itself with callous, reckless cruelty, emboldened by his independence and fascinated with the power he held over me. Wracked by guilt over our poverty and

5

annoyed by his failed attempts to find work, he'd grown bitter and took it out on me. It all changed one night when he snapped while we were fighting in our dirty, miserable apartment and hit me on the cheek.

Weeping, I called my parents for help. They were adamant that I needed to figure this out on my own. Belinda didn't even pick up my calls or answer my texts for help. But Trevor...he had me make a promise. He'd send me all the savings Mom and Dad had put aside for him if only I'd leave Derrick and start a new life somewhere else. I was twenty years old then. I'd taken my chances and left Derrick in the night. A new life was waiting for me, and I took my chances, one after another, until I had a life I could be proud of. And now I was right back here.

Funny how life turns out, isn't it?

"I heard things," said Trevor. "Little bits here and there. I remember when I finally got LinkedIn and looked you up. I couldn't believe it!"

I smiled. After I left Derrick, I'd taken a train to Boston and spent a year working as a maid in motels and rich people's houses, saving every penny I could, surviving off cereal in a dingy apartment. Eventually, I took a few courses, leading to university and certifications. It was enough for me to qualify as a childminder. I'd worked as a nanny, and an *au pair* in Boston for a while then moved to New York. The same thing always...a year here, a year there. When the opportunity came, I went overseas to Switzerland, where they paid good money for people like me. How quickly ten years had gone by. While looking after the spoiled children of an ambassador family in Geneva, I saw an ad I couldn't believe. A residential position on Criker's Isle for Max Fircress, entrepreneur.

"So where to, sis?"

Trevor's low voice boomed in the small cabin.

"Fairview."

Trevor whistled through his teeth when I told him that.

"Wow. You working for Max? That's gonna be a difficult house to live in."

"Why? Because of the whole...wife thing?" A little Googling had revealed that Max was a widower. His wife, Winifred, had died in a car accident three years ago, leaving behind a daughter, now nine years old.

Trevor scanned the horizon, a faraway look in his eye. He obviously wanted to say something, but he shook it off.

"That was real tragic," he said quickly.

"Have you seen the kid?" I asked.

"I have, I guess," said Trevor. "Kid's got behavioral issues. And she doesn't talk."

I nodded. So it was common knowledge. *Severe behavioral issues, selective mutism.* The words had rung like alarm bells on the ad. Mindy, Max's daughter, was evidently a troubled case. I wasn't sure what was waiting for me at Fairview, the house Max had built for his now-dead wife on the Northern side of town. But despite all my trepidation and fear, I couldn't help but be called back to Cricker's Isle. My home.

Why now? I didn't know.

As we climbed the hills on the other side of town, I could see the lights of the mansion coming into view. Max was a billionaire, and the house was a sleek, modern design, a large square construction with a balcony running around the first floor and tall, high chimneys protruding from the second. I'd seen an article that morning about the inspiration behind the build. It had meant to be a statement of the principles by which Max ran his furniture business, the one which had made him a billionaire. It was sustainable, almost entirely self-sufficient, with solar and wind power built into its design. Now, I reflected. It was a sad monument to a shattered home and a traumatized child.

The day before my interview on Zoom, I'd thumbed through a few pictures of Max as I packed to leave. He looked strong, with broad shoulders. Not one for suits, he was wearing a simple, plaid shirt in most of Fircress Furniture's publicity. He had a strong jaw with the gentle beginnings of stubble and a thick head of black hair. But when we'd interviewed, I'd been shocked. The man before me didn't look nearly as muscular. In fact, he looked practically wasted away. The stubble was overgrown, and though he still looked handsome, he looked his thirty-eight years. I could see I was dealing with a different man from the one Criker's Isle had known and loved. I'd heard he was disfigured in the accident too, but if that was true, I couldn't tell.

These gloomy thoughts were interrupted by a note of warning in Trevor's voice. I noticed he'd been happily chattering away on the drive while I brooded on the past.

"There's something I've gotta tell you," he said as we pulled up at the driveway of Fairview.

"Huh?" I replied, staring at the high stretch of hedges surrounding the property on all sides.

"Well, it's about him. Derrick, that is."

My eyes widened, and I turned to face him. "He's here?"

"Yeah. He came back. He's well…" I looked at Trevor. I could already see what he was going to say. "Derrick's the sheriff around here."

My blood ran cold. "How in the hell did that bastard end up becoming sheriff?"

"Long story. I guess Officer Park must have liked him. After you...well, after Derrick went out on his own, I guess he must have joined the police because he got reassigned to Criker a coupla of years ago. Officer Park died last year, and Derrick's been running the place since then. Look, sis, there's no love lost between us, but I think he's calmed down now. Probably won't even remember you."

I doubted that and tried to shake off my fears as I opened the passenger door of Trevor's cruiser. "Thanks for the lift, Trevor. I get to have visitors here, you know. You're welcome anytime."

He nodded, smiling, though I could see that in his eyes, there was a tinge of guilt at not being able to return the favor. "I still live with Mom and Dad, remodeled the garage and all," he said. "Belinda...has her own place." We both knew what that meant. I clearly wasn't welcome at either home. "Look, I'll give you my new number. You'll call me, won't you?"

I retrieved my phone and keyed in his digits before saving it and jumping out of the truck. "You're the best, Trevor."

He lowered the window and leaned toward me as I walked away from the truck.

"Hey, sis," he said. "We live in hope. Remember that?"

I nodded. He'd said that to me ten years ago, the last time we talked. I thought at the time that the kid was wise beyond his years.

"I love you, Trevor," I said. "Sorry for getting rain and mud all over your seats. Come see me, okay?"

As his car pulled out of the driveway and started to make its way into town, I looked at the enormous, quiet house before me and made my way up to the front door.

Chapter 2

Max

"Miss Gardner will be here soon, Min."

Nothing.

"You want a snack before she comes?"

Not a sound.

"Mindy?"

She didn't even turn her head—just sat staring at the sketchbook in her hands. It was like she didn't even know I was there.

I sighed and sat down at my desk. Since Winnie passed, I'd moved my office into the living room, where Mindy could play or sit when she felt like it. I searched the horizon through the wide window, my eyes shifting across the landscape as rain and sea spray battered the land. I felt the old familiar pain running across my chest and put my hand there to feel the scar. It seemed to vibrate against me. The pain flared less as time passed, but I always knew it was there. It was something I could never escape.

We'd been driving in the night when it happened. Suddenly

I'd lost control for reasons I didn't understand even now. It was raining at the time, but not like now. It was a storm. Even still, I had no one else to blame.

When the brakes failed, and the car slid off the road on the way down from Fairview, I had no one else to blame.

When it rolled down a set of rocks, I had no one else to blame.

When my wife, Winnie, was killed on impact with a tree, I had no one else to blame.

And all the therapy, the shrinks, and the damned grief counseling could never change my mind about that. Or about my daughter. Because since Winnie had died, Mindy hadn't said a word. And I had no one else to blame for that, either.

The doorbell rang, interrupting my self-pity. I got up, walked through the house, past the kitchen and breakfast bar, and into the lobby. A frail silhouette stood outside.

It happened every time. I imagined it might be her, that the past three years might have been a nightmare, and I'd open the door to find Winnie, maybe late from the office. "Don't leave me standing out here all day!" she'd say, and I'd laugh and hold her to me because my wife wasn't dead, just late from the office. And every time I opened the door and found someone there, a delivery guy or someone from Fairtown, I'd get my heart broken again, just a little bit.

But I froze when I saw Sophie Gardner standing on my doorstep.

She looked younger than I had seen on Zoom and was drenched head to toe. "Miss Gardner? You are here. I wasn't expecting you until later on." I looked at my watch and then back at her. "You should have said something. I would have sent a cab to pick you up—"

"That's alright, Mr. Fircress," she said.

"Max, please," I replied as I helped her with her sodden raincoat. "We don't stand on ceremony at Fairview."

She kneeled and undid the laces on her walking boots, obviously prepared for the rain. As I watched her crouch in the lobby, I couldn't help but notice her athleticism. She looked strong and nimble as her fingers quickly worked the laces, and she spanned around to place the shoes by the doorway. She looked strong in all the places I felt weak, young in all the ways I felt old.

"And where..." she said, "...is *Miss* Fircress?"

"Mindy's just through here," I said as we passed through the hallway and kitchen. "You'll have to forgive the layout of the house. Winnie was...well, my wife was very particular when we built it."

"I think it's lovely," she said. Sophie Gardner had a soft, warm voice that raised a spark of feeling in me. Despite her somber dress and serious attitude, the house seemed a little warmer and brighter for having her in it.

As we entered the living room, I saw Mindy.

"Here she is," I said. "She probably won't respond to you, not for a few days anyway."

A few weeks, even more, I thought.

Sophie kneeled in front of Mindy by the fireplace. She waited.

After a while, maybe thirty seconds, Mindy realized someone was there, someone unfamiliar. She looked up.

"Hi. I'm Sophie. What's your name?"

Mindy only shrugged, her attention reverting to what she was doing before we walked in. Sophie stood and approached me.

"Not a word? Not even hello or goodbye?"

"Not since her mother passed," I said. "She was bright. I know she still is. She can still read and does her schoolwork well enough, given that she only goes twice a week. But she doesn't talk. Have you seen anything like that before?"

"Selective mutism happens for a lot of reasons," Sophie said. "I can tell you what the textbooks say. But the truth is often more complicated. What she needs is time. And not to be rushed."

"I don't expect you to work miracles, Miss Gardner. I just need someone to look after her. Honestly, it's...it's been a rough few years for both of us. I appreciate whatever help you can give. And I'll pay whatever you ask, just for the help. Just—"

She nodded and smiled at me, a warm, wide-eyed smile that seemed to see all the pain I was feeling and say *it's okay, it's going to be okay*. I had been about to tell her not to give up on us, but I didn't need to. I was impressed by her presence. Sophie was so peaceful to be around. She was one of the most qualified people I interviewed for the job and was a true professional, which can be a rarity when it comes to a job as vocational as childcare.

"Truth is..." Sophie said, "...what Mindy might need is a friend. I'd love to be that friend for her. That person who's always going to be there."

I nodded. "We need a friend. I mean..." I said, correcting myself hastily, "...*she* needs a friend."

"You both do," replied Sophie. I felt a little ashamed, but she took my hand. Hers was warm and comforting. I felt softened by the simple kindness she showed me.

"Well, I'd better get my things unpacked," she said.

***

Night had already fallen, and the rain had finally stopped by the time I had shown Sophie to her room and she'd unpacked. She returned just when the casserole for dinner was ready. I plated the food and watched as Mindy picked at her food, Sophie watching her carefully.

"Maybe you two can get acquainted while I'm gone?" I said.

"Won't you eat?" Sophie asked, concerned.

"Later..." I smiled at her concern. I wanted Sophie and Mindy to eat and get acquainted as I'd be getting back to the swing of things at my company in a few days. I wanted Mindy to be comfortable enough as we transitioned into Sophie being her full-time carer.

Mindy didn't move a muscle as I left the dining area, grabbed my coat, and walked out into the chilly evening ambiance.

I walked a lot. I find it helped my pain and gave me time to think. It was the first time I'd done it at night for a while—I was typically tied to Mindy whenever she wasn't at school or when my housekeeper, Mrs. Langley, wasn't around to watch her. As long as you didn't physically encroach on her space or force her to do anything, Mindy never acted up or ran away. Day after day, she sat around, doing nothing. I'd put all my hopes on Sophie to do what was right and made a mental note not to pile any more pressure.

As I rounded the hilltop and looked down at Fairview, I felt almost normal as the lights twinkled below me, making the house appear like a ship sailing on a distant, dark ocean. My eyes were drawn to the living room as Sophie appeared at the window. She looked out, the soft lights framing her gentle face. She seemed pensive. Her green eyes crinkled at the corners. I found myself wanting to know what she was thinking, if she was up to the task, if she would stay and be there for Mindy.

Or me.

Then a small smile stretched her bow-shaped lips, and a puff of air left my lungs. Her auburn hair swished to the side as she turned away, maybe to talk to Mindy. I shook my thoughts away, feeling a little guilty about spying on her without her knowing, and quickly walked on.

It didn't get lost on me how the feeling of loneliness was particularly poignant today.

Nearly half an hour later, I was walking back down the hill when I got a call on my cell phone.

"Max? It's Winston here. How are you, brother-of-mine?"

"Hey, Winston. How're things in Boston?"

"Absolutely fantastic, old man. How are you and Little Miss Mindy?"

I hated it when he called her that, in that phony way. But my brother-in-law calling me was always a good sign. It meant that things were going well. Winston didn't call when things weren't going well. He'd stepped up and ran the business for the last two years when I couldn't. When Winnie died, her shares had gone half to me and half to Winston, her twin brother, as per her will. And we'd done our best to honor her by running the business true to the principles we'd founded it on.

I'd taken Winston on at Winnie's request when it became clear that none of the hair-brained ideas his parents had funded would come good. He'd been a hard worker, reliable, and even a little ambitious. Now Winnie's investment in Winston was paying off. Our profit margin was increasing, and Fircress Furniture's stock price was climbing slowly. I'd made enough money for a lifetime and was more interested in the sustainability of the business and spreading the message, but Winston's enthusiasm still made me happy.

"We're just fine, Winston. Still planning on heading over

tomorrow?"

"If that's alright with you, Maxy-boy. Say, how's that new nanny? Did you say she was local or something?"

"Yeah. Well, I'll see you tomorrow, Winston."

I put the phone down, and my eyes traced past Fairview to the guesthouse, which perched on a rock. With two bedrooms and its own garage, it was mainly used as Winston's home-away-from-home when he wanted to come and see me.

Below me, movement on the hill distracted me. I backed up the track a little. From here, I could see through a gap in the hedge where I could swear a figure was standing, waiting. I blinked and took a step forward, but when I focused on the dense pine hedge, I noticed it was gone, and the house lay still and quiet in the cold.

Must be the lights and shadows, I thought as I continued back home.

I walked down the track but stopped when I got back to the house. A police car was sitting at the bottom of the driveway, parked exactly over the boundary line. Derrick was thumbing absentmindedly through his notebook when he saw me round the hedges.

"How ya doin', Max?" Derrick said.

"Just fine, thanks, Derrick," I said. I smiled thinly at him. I never liked that guy and didn't vote for him to be sheriff. But I was willing to let bygones be bygones, except he always turned up where he wasn't wanted.

"Had any more trouble with them raccoons?" asked Derrick.

"I don't think there was much trouble in the first place," I replied.

Derrick nodded as though he wasn't paying much attention.

"Uh huh, uh huh," he said. He was chewing something—gum or something. That was a habit I could never stand.

"Say, Max," Derrick said. "Little bird told me you got Sophie Gardner doin' your childcare for ya?"

"Oh yeah?" I said. "Who told you that?"

He didn't answer me. "She up there now?" he said, casting his eyes absentmindedly towards the house.

I stepped past him, past the car where he was leaning, and into the driveway. "I'll be honest, *sheriff*. I'm not really sure how it's any of your business if she is."

Derrick laughed, revealing his teeth. "Relax, Max. Me and Sophie, we go *way* back. Tell her I said hi, will you?"

I nodded politely and walked back to my house.

"And oh, Max?" said Derrick. "I only mention those raccoons because if you don't do something about them, that could come back to you..." The sheriff fixed his belt, jaw snapping as he chewed. "Legally, I mean."

"Thanks for the tip, Derrick," I said. "Goodnight."

Chapter 3

Sophie

I'd been at Fairview for the past three days, mostly observing. And as soon as I saw her with that sketchbook, I knew what to do. Kids are always telling us what they need. I think we forget that sometimes. But, if you think about it, we have evolved to ask for what we need to survive. And kids were great at that.

So when I saw Mindy with that sketchbook, I knew just what she needed.

After Max left for the day, I put the pencil in her hand and sat by with a cup of coffee. At first, Mindy looked at it, not really knowing what to do. But I could tell the blank page fascinated her. She wasn't zoning out, escaping from it all. She was trying to find something in there.

At first, she made a few tiny scratches with the pencil.

Then, she drew a circle. I watched it become a sun as the lines around it spread.

"What's that?" I said.

She looked at me and said nothing.

"Is it something in the sky?" I said.

She nodded.

"Is it big?"

She nodded again. She knew exactly what I was saying. Her listening skills were intact. Maybe even up to speed for a nine-year-old.

"Want to color it in?" I gave her a choice of red and yellow pencils. She took both, shading the outside of the circle red and the inside yellow.

"I like that," I said. "It's really pretty."

I smiled as I looked at the pretty little girl with black, curly hair drawing happily away. There was nothing wrong with her, as far as I was concerned. The capacity to speak and understand was there. Trust was what Mindy needed. And I was going to do my best to give it to her. I sat with her for another hour until I noticed my empty coffee cup.

I got up and walked into the kitchen. As I entered, I saw a man standing by the fridge, his long arms reaching to replace something. I screamed and dropped my cup. As it shattered on the floor, he jumped, then laughed.

"Oh Lord, I am sorry. I was only getting a snack...must have startled you. Didn't Max mention I was coming today?"

I breathed an enormous sigh of relief. "Goodness me, I apologize. You must be Mr. Locklow. I'm Sophie, the nanny." I stepped over to shake his hand.

"That's me, ma'am. I am indeed Winston Locklow. And Mr. Locklow is my father, so I would appreciate it if you'd just call me Winston."

The man shaking my hand was bony and tall and spoke with

the merest hint of a southern drawl. He wore a baggy, cream suit and pants, and a blue shirt. Atop his large forehead was a crop of black hair, which was thinning despite the fact he couldn't have been a day over forty—if Winnie had been alive, she'd be thirty-three. His face, likewise, looked a little pinched and old, and his eyes were quite dark, almost black. So this was Winston Locklow, Max's brother-in-law, business partner, and (now) sole heir to the Locklow fortune. I bent down to clear up the fragments of the coffee-stained cup while he spoke.

"I really ought to have called before, but I just couldn't wait to get here. How is your young charge, Miss Gardner?"

I didn't have much of a chance to speak, as before I knew it, he'd brushed right past me, sauntering through the house as though it were his own. I was a little unnerved. I'd read a few things about the Locklows guiltily on my phone last night before I went to bed. I knew Winston hadn't been very successful before Max brought him into the business. I also knew that Winston had started buying and selling land in recent years. I wondered how he possibly had the time to do that *and* work with Fircress Furniture. I threw the remains of my mug in a bin and wandered through.

"There she is!" I heard him say from the other room. "Little Miss Mindy! Little bit old to be drawing suns and moons, aren't we?"

I stepped into the living room, where Winston crouched over Mindy. He put his hand on her head and ruffled her hair. Mindy didn't seem to like the attention much.

"Today, we've been drawing to explain how we feel, haven't we, Mindy?" I said. Maybe she'd talk to him.

Winston stood and peered at me. He seemed almost amused at the way I spoke. "Well, I hope you can teach her to draw something a little better than that. I mean, looks like something a toddler would do, doesn't it?"

If I winced, he didn't notice. I knew Mindy could understand everything he was saying. As if in response, Mindy closed her sketchbook. I sighed at that. It was going to be hard to get her started again.

"Now, I hope you will forgive me, Miss, uh, Gardner, was it?" Winston said, brushing past me. "But I have to unpack my things in the guesthouse. The cab driver wouldn't even unpack my bags. People in this town need a reckoning, don't they? *Ciao*! That's Italian for *goodbye*, by the way."

With that, he closed the door of the house behind him, and I saw him through the living room window, his lanky frame ascending the hill in big strides. I was glad the man would be staying half a mile away from me. I couldn't explain why, but something in his manner just seemed off.

I turned to Mindy.

"I don't know what he's talking about," I said. "I love your drawings."

***

Max wasn't back that evening. I knew he wanted us to have some time alone, but I was having difficulty getting used to being up here alone. Mindy was napping on the sofa while I made dinner in the kitchen. I hadn't managed to persuade her to stray far from the house, but she'd been tempted into the driveway to look at the trees. My eyes wandered nervously to the main road the whole time. Even as it grew dark, I nervously scanned the treeline through the kitchen window.

I wanted to text Max and ask when he'd be back. Truth was, I didn't feel all that comfortable knowing where Derrick was. Was it possible he might come looking for me?

Ten years ago, when we'd lived together, I'd begged him for the money I was making working at a 7/11, hoping he'd let me leave, let me go away. I remembered his raised voice, back against the wall, the punch that sent me sprawling on the floor, and his words. *Wherever you go, I'll come find you. I'll never let you go.* That last awful night was behind me. But the words had stayed with me for years. And now, without knowing it, I'd stumbled right back into a town that he protected. The thought that my first boyfriend, a raging ball of hatred, was in a position of power...

It made me feel sick to contemplate. But then, I noticed a figure moving in the trees, and I jumped out of my skin.

Whoever it was, they were spying on the house. I dialed Trevor's number.

"Sophie? You okay?"

"Trevor. Listen. There's someone in the front garden. At Fairview. Max flew to the mainland, and I can see Winston's silhouette from here up in the guesthouse."

"You sure?" said Trevor incredulously.

"Trevor, I just need to know. Is Derrick out right now? Could it be him?"

Trevor sighed. "Sis, that's crazy. No way he'd do a thing like that."

"Are you sure? Do you know where he is right now?"

"Sophie, I can see him right now. He's in his office."

"Then who's in the damn garden?" I was almost yelling at him. The figure in the trees was creeping me out. It looked misshapen and strange in the blue ending of the twilight.

"I don't know. Look, I'll go up and check it out."

"I'll see for myself."

"Sophie, do not go out there. If there's an intruder, you should stay inside and—"

I hung up. Slipping my boots on, I burst out of the front door and made it halfway down the grass hill towards the raised beds at the top of the driveway. It was a steep angle, and I got down there quick enough, even though I could see the figure was trying to slink towards the gate.

"Whoever's there, I can see you. So you better turn around now!"

The figure stopped, and I heard it sigh. As it came into the light, I realized it was a woman in a puffed windbreaker. She took down her hood. I would have recognized that face anywhere.

"Belinda?" I said. "Is that you?"

She rolled her eyes. "Yeah."

"What...what are you doing here?"

Belinda shrugged.

"Are you okay?"

"I'm just fine." There was silence between us. Then she spoke again. "So you're looking after Mindy Fircress?"

I nodded.

"Are you responsible enough for that? I hear she's a pretty messed-up kid."

Everything in my brain told me to yell at her for saying that, but I resisted. She'd always looked down at me. "I've worked as a qualified nanny for seven years, Bee. You might have known that if you'd asked."

"A nanny?" she said. "Is that even a career?"

"Beats working wherever you are working I'm sure...still at the Fairtown Costco, aren't you? Sure you are."

She sneered at me. "Glad to see things are working out so well you had to come home. You know, I should tell Max about your old boyfriend. He'd be so impressed with his new nanny."

I sighed. I was too exhausted for any of this. "Say hi to Mom for me, Bee. Oh, and if I see you on Max's property again without his permission, I'll call the police."

She said nothing in response but clicked her tongue and turned around.

I watched her break through the treeline and join the main road before I went back inside.

I texted Trevor. *It was Belinda, if u can believe it*

Oh...what she want?

No clue. At least it ain't a thief or something.

Yeah...do u mind if I come over tomorrow morning? Would Max mind? Trevor replied.

Sure. Tomorrow morning should be ok. Why tho? I wrote back.

Something I want to talk about with u.

Chapter 4

Max

"There's something you should know," Sophie said when I got home.

"Oh yeah?" I said. "Winston got here okay?"

"Oh, just fine. He's up in the guesthouse now." Sophie undid her ponytail, as she usually did when Mindy was in bed. She was disciplined and professional. It was like now she could take off the mask she'd worn during the day and be herself again. I understood that so well, and it made me feel a strange kinship with her, as though we were connected, even by the loosest threads. As I watched her shake out her auburn hair, I felt a rush of something and then guiltily suppressed it as she carried on talking.

"I'll need some time tomorrow morning. Trevor, my brother, is coming over."

"Your brother? You know, people love that kid. He's gonna make a great sheriff one day. Beats Derrick, the other guy, for sure!"

Sophie smiled thinly, but her gorgeous green eyes darted away. I followed her glance to the kitchen window, the driveway.

I could tell she was hiding something, and I didn't want to beat around the bush.

"You know him, don't you?" I said. "Derrick, I mean."

Sophie looked away. I could tell there was something. "Yeah, I do."

I reached out and put a hand on her shoulder. She seemed startled and turned to me. As she did, I realized her confident exterior had collapsed. She looked younger and frightened, like a wounded animal. But when she met my eyes and saw me smiling, she relaxed. "You'll tell me when you're ready, Sophie," I said quietly. "I trust you. Mindy trusts you. Never seen her get off to sleep so peacefully. It's been a few days, but you're doing a great job. You know that?"

That look in her eyes—that wounded animal look—vanished. She was back to her old self again. "I...thank you, Max. But that's not all. My sister came up here. Uninvited. Truth is, we had a falling out years ago before I left. My mom and I don't speak. And Belinda and me, well, we've never really gotten along."

I nodded as she opened up to me about her family situation, but a creeping feeling continued climbing along my neck.

Belinda.

Everything catches up with us in the end.

***

I stayed close to home the next day, watching over Mindy for a few hours in the morning, and giving Sophie some time off to spend time with Trevor. After she came back, I stayed around but gave her and Mindy their space. I was enchanted by the way Sophie was with Mindy. She was patient and dedicated but gave her full attention. It was like she knew Mindy. I hadn't seen anyone look after her that way since Winnie.

I sat in the living room and worked for most of the day. It had been so long since I'd been able to give the business my full attention, and there were a mountain of reports and files, quarterly statements that I hadn't reviewed. I didn't like that. What would Winnie have said if she'd seen how I left things? I texted Winston and told him I'd come up and see him after lunch.

We ate a late lunch together, and Mindy actually seemed interested in her food for once. She was different from how she'd been before Sophie, smiling and happy. I couldn't help but smile at Sophie when I saw how happy my daughter looked. After they ate, they went to play in the driveway. I went up to see Winston. I ascended the hill using the old farmer's track and saw the front door. There was a note there:

Dearest Max,

Sorry very much, old pal, but I have had to go out to Pointer's Rock for the day. Shan't be back until sundown. Give my regards to L.M.M.

- Winston.

I don't know why, but it was only then that my scar started to sear and burn again for the first time in a few days. I made a note to call my doctor about it and decided to go and do a grocery run instead. I couldn't imagine what Winston was doing at Pointer's Rock, on the far side of the island, but I was happy he was out there all the same. He'd never seemed very interested in Criker's Isle until Winnie had passed away.

I drove down the main road and crossed the bridge into Fairtown. I passed ramshackle houses and gray, featureless apartment blocks. Each time I went, my heart sank to see the deprivation the town had suffered. Big business had tried to come to Criker's Isle a few times, but each time, promises were broken. When loans arrived for fishermen, the quotas dashed their hopes. When tourism came to the island, it promised rejuvenation and money for the locals, only for a resort to be built on the other side of the island, smack bang in the nature reserve. Local laws had fortunately prevented the rest of the island's Eastern side from being swallowed up by development, but the real cruelty was that most of the work was seasonal. Now, at the start of Fall, no one was coming to Criker's Isle for their vacation. I was miserable to see the island my wife had loved so much suffer like this. There was surely some way to help the town, and I made a note to ask Winston about it when I saw him.

Business is about giving back, after all.

My dad said that to me when I was very young. He was a carpenter back on the mainland, and I was in his workshop as soon as I could walk. That was where my interest in furniture started, but it wasn't just that. My dad taught me all kinds of things about sourcing wood, working in a way that wasn't wasteful, and running a fair business that employed good people and paid an honest day's wage. Fircress Furniture was founded on those principles. He'd died when I was small, but I still remembered little things about him, like the way sawdust gathered on his hands and how he smelled of varnish and pine when he came home in the evenings.

It took me less than ten minutes to get to the only large supermarket in Fairtown. I headed inside and began throwing some stuff in the trolley, double-checking the list I had in hand. Sophie insisted on making mine and Mindy's lunch, but I'd reminded her that she was a nanny, not a cook. Dinner was my responsibility, and I was making chicken pie for them. It had been Mindy's favorite when she was little and first starting to eat proper food. Besides, it gave Sophie and her more time to play.

As I rounded a corner in the supermarket, looking for something for Mindy's school lunches, I heard a voice behind me, and my heart sank.

"Max?" It was Belinda.

"Hi, Belinda," I said, turning and smiling weakly as she stepped towards me.

"How are you doing? How's Mindy?"

I gritted my teeth. I could never leave well enough alone.

"What were you doing at the house yesterday, Belinda? You scared your sister."

"She told you? Figures." She frowned, and her eyes flashed with anger. Pulling her hair across her face, she turned and looked at the shelves, trying to seem casual. "Wasn't trying to scare her. I just wanted to see what she was up to at Fairview. You don't know her, Max. Not like me."

"I know enough to know I trust her, Belinda. I can't say that for everyone."

"What's that supposed to mean?" Her outraged tone drew the eye of a few shoppers nearby, and I tried to calm her down. But she wouldn't be calm. "I want what's best for you, Max. Has she told you why she even left the island in the first place?"

"Belinda—" I started, remembering the bits and pieces Sophie had shared with me in confidence.

"Don't you *Belinda* me," she said. "I used to think you were different, Max."

"Now, what's going on here?" said a familiar voice. I tried not to let a groan escape my lips. "I'm sure whatever it is, we can discuss it like adults," said Derrick.

"Nothing's the matter," I said. "We were just having a discussion."

"I'm sure whatever Belinda had to say..." said Derrick, "...is worth hearing." He had a smug smile. He always did whenever people were at odds with one another. I hated that. Clearly, even Belinda couldn't stand the sight of Derrick.

"I'm sure..." I said slowly, "...that it was a private conversation."

"It's always a private conversation before the law's concerned, Mr. Fircress." If I wasn't mistaken, Derrick was practically threatening me.

"Cut it out, Derrick," hissed Belinda. "God knows you've done enough where my family's concerned." She turned on her heels and walked away quickly, her shoes clacking down the supermarket aisle.

"You seem to be making a lot of folks upset lately, Max," said Derrick. "Understandable, of course. But it doesn't make for a happy town."

"Nor does the rate at which you're charging fines, Derrick," I replied. "It's not like people around here can afford it." I regretted that almost as soon as I said it.

"Well, I'm sure some billionaire hiding up the hill in his mansion would know a lot about that," said Derrick. The fake smile had disappeared from his face, and he was standing close to me. I knew any confrontation between the sheriff and me wouldn't end well.

"If you don't mind, I've got to get home."

"Sure, sure. I bet Sophie and Mindy are wondering where you've gone to. Did you tell her I said hi, by the way?"

I wanted to tell him to take my daughter's name out of his damned dirty mouth but thought better of it and went to the cashier.

Chapter 5

Sophie

Lately, I couldn't help but look at Max—when he bent to inspect the piping on his eco-burner, or in the kitchen as he chopped vegetables, or stood at the stove, lit by the light of the fan. I looked at him, and something in my heart leaped with a secret longing.

It was wrong, I know. But as I saw him stroke his beard or stretch his broad shoulders in the mornings, I sensed him coming back to life, imbued with some new strength or resolve. I had such a tiny part to play in his life; I knew that. And as much as Mindy was responding to me and coming out of her shell, I felt ashamed, knowing I was a poor substitute for the mother who'd once walked the floors of Fairview. And I burned with secret guilt because of what Trevor had told me the other day.

Trevor drove over the morning after Belinda had literally crept back into my life. We'd taken a walk on the hills and watched the sunrise, talking about Winnie. I wanted to know about her. I think because I wanted to know more about Max and Mindy. Whatever Trevor wanted to tell me had been about her as well.

"She was nice. Pretty, kinda funny. She had a real...real personality. She reminded me of you, Sophie."

"How did it happen, Trevor? How did she die? Like the real reason. So many conflicting stories on the internet, and I can't bring myself to ask Max. I couldn't."

"Seems like you two have really hit it off, huh?"

"And Mindy. She's my focus. Poor kid just needs someone with her. She'll open up. I know it."

Trevor paused and began to talk in a low voice.

"I need to talk to you about the accident. They were on their way back from the airstrip. It was a bad night, practically a storm. Though nothing like the one we had after you left, Sophie. Practically destroyed the place. Anyway, Max's brakes failed. I don't know why. God, that car was new. It wasn't like it had bad plates or anything. It spun off the side of the road and down onto the rocks. Happened not too far from where I picked you up last week."

I shuddered. Poor Max.

"Anyway, he came pretty close to dying himself. Winnie was killed instantly. Would have felt nothing. That's what the coroner said. Mind you, they always say that. Helps make it easier sometimes, you know. But..."

"But what?" I said. I knew that look in Trevor's eyes, even though it had been so long since we'd lived under the same roof. He never could resist an unanswered question. Even when he was little, I'd find him asking dad all kinds of things. *Dad, how high can a seagull fly? Dad, how does a plane land without crashing?* I never guessed his love of mystery would land him a job at the sheriff's office.

"The truth is, I always thought there was something up with that crash," said Trevor. *"The report's awful. Derrick's never written them*

well. But Lord, it was patchy. There wasn't even any information on the car."

"Derrick investigated the crash?" I said, eyes wide.

"Well, sure. He was a Deputy at the time and the first on the scene. It was his call. They ruled it an accident, and we chose not to investigate. I was just back from my training on the mainland then. They wouldn't even let me touch the file at the time."

"Have you ever told Max that?"

Trevor shook his head. "Of course not. Damn, Sophie. It could cost me my job. Still, I never understood what went on there."

"Trevor, will you do something for me?"

He nodded. "Anything for you, sis."

"Try and understand."

We parted that morning, and I returned to the house where Mindy was scribbling on a sketchpad, Max zoned in on his laptop. He hadn't called me since then, but what he told me during that walk kept me curious about what had really happened on the night Max had lost his wife and Mindy, her mother.

***

"You're a real hero, you know that?" said Max to me. I was taking a well-earned rest after a difficult day with Mindy. She'd had a meltdown in the morning after dropping her bowl of cereal. The sight of it had sent her crazy, clawing in a frenzy. I had to pull her out from under the table and hold her until the crying stopped. She'd recovered in the afternoon and done some drawing for me. She was getting good now, drawing people and places. Even I was starting to be featured. I always appeared in the same boring blue dress I'd worn on our first day together, with "SOFIE" written next to me in pink letters. Max loved it.

"I'm certainly not a hero," I said. I wished I could tell Max what Trevor had told me, but it risked too much. Our friendship was growing. When Mindy was asleep, we were always together, usually while I read a book and he pottered away in the living room. His presence brought me peace and safety. It had been so long since I'd been in a man's presence and felt safe and comforted rather than anxious.

Plus, it was purely conjecture at this point. I wasn't going to rip open, or continue to rip, wounds based on baseless information.

"Well, since Mrs. Langley's in this evening, I'd like to take you out for dinner and say thanks," said Max.

"Oh, Max, no," I said quickly. "I'm just doing my job."

"We both know you're doing more than that," he said. "And I like you, Sophie. You've brought something into my home I didn't know it could have."

What did he mean by that? I don't know, but it made something in me purr with delight. I felt appreciated. Max always knew how to make me feel appreciated. Nothing was taken for granted by him.

"I guess we could go out," I said.

"I thought I could take you to Giardino's," he said. That was an Italian restaurant on the waterfront. It was the fanciest place in town. I'd never been as a kid, of course. It was way too expensive.

"Max, that's way too pricey," I said. "You can't take me there."

"C'mon, Sophie. It's my treat. Okay. You tell me where you'd like to go."

I thought about it for a moment. "I guess we could go to Bushey's if you like."

Bushey's was a diner halfway up the hill between Fairtown and the airstrip. The view was gorgeous, but that wasn't really why I wanted to go there. Before Derrick, before everything, before I'd had to leave, Bushey's had been my family's favorite place to eat. Our monthly trips on Saturdays were always fun. Trevor and I would both have chowder and poke fun at Belinda, who, deep in the grip of teenage angst, would pick over a salad while Mom and Dad argued.

"The diner?" Max asked. He thought about it for a second. "Okay. Bushey's it is."

Half an hour later, Max was holding the door open for me.

The diner was smaller than I remembered as Max and I climbed the steps to enter the tiny aluminum trailer. It was still spotlessly clean on the inside, but there looked to be some fraying around the red leather seats. An outbuilding on the back housed the kitchen.

The woman at the counter was wearing one of those dresses from the fifties, though I was mercifully glad to see the staff no longer had to wear those paper sailboat hats. We took a seat, and the waitress came over. She poured me a coffee. Max asked for green tea, but they brought him chamomile. He didn't know I'd noticed until he caught me giggling.

"Guess this is all they had," he said, grinning and taking a sip. It was the first time I'd seen him really have fun and enjoy himself since we'd met. I felt privileged to be in his company and safe and snug inside the booth of the diner. But something had been nagging at me, and I had to ask.

"What happened yesterday at the store? You seemed kind of down when you got back."

Max's eyes glazed over, and he ran a hand through his thick hair, ruffling it a little and making him look even more handsome. It was light and warm inside the diner, but a little chill was already in the air.

"As it happens, I had a conversation with our local sheriff."

I felt a shiver run down my spine. "I can only imagine how charming Derrick must be now that he's enforcing the law *and* being a jerk at the same time."

"From how you talk about him, either he swept you off your feet or ruined your life."

"I guess it was both," I replied. I was going to have to tell Max sooner or later, and I sure didn't want to be beaten to it by Belinda. Or Derrick himself. "We were young when we fell in love. Soon fell out of it, too. But not before he dragged me to the mainland, isolated me from every family member who'd still talk to me, and cut off access to my salary."

Max's mouth practically opened in disbelief. "And this guy's the sheriff?" he said. "No wonder this town's screwed."

"Don't say that," I said, a little afraid of the pessimistic tone in his voice. "I know it can be better. And God knows I know it isn't perfect. My own family is afraid to tell each other when they speak to me. But I believe this place has a lot of good. I'm happy you're here to help."

"I've been meaning to help for a long time," said Max carefully. "But lately, things haven't exactly been easy."

The waitress came over, and we ordered our food. I was um-ing and ah-ing over whether to get a chicken-fried steak or a salad bowl, but Max decided before me. "Two chicken-fried steaks. Two salad bowls," he said. He winked at me as the waitress scribbled our order down and left. "I've never eaten here before, but I'm willing to bet that's more of a side salad."

I laughed when he said that, and then, suddenly, I felt it. I felt myself blush a little and warm inside, and something brave in me admitted it to myself. *You like him. And he's a good man.* What exactly my brain intended me to do with that information, I didn't know. But I was excited.

"Why did you decide to look after kids?" said Max out of the blue.

"I guess I feel pretty complicated about how my parents were with me," I said. "A lot of people feel uncomfortable about another adult getting close to their child, but most of my good memories are either of my grandparents or my aunts and uncles. Or here," I reflected, looking around the little diner wistfully. "I just want to make a difference. If one child feels stronger, safer, happier because I'm around, it's enough."

Max gleamed. "Well, you're making a difference for Mindy."

I smiled. "She keeps drawing pictures of me! But I don't want her to draw pictures of me. I want her to draw pictures of you. Or pictures of...her mom."

Max looked intently at me. I saw him study my face. Was he probing me to see if I really meant that? I couldn't tell. Either way, what he said next made my heart dance on a string.

"When I see her with you, I see her coming back to the way she was before Winnie passed. And I love that. I really do, Sophie. And it means the world to me."

Was it just my imagination, or was there something else in his voice? Something beyond praise, admiration, and gratitude. Was it a note of tenderness that made him lower his voice, made it husky and soft and in the warm light of the diner? I don't know, but I realized that Max was the nicest, cleverest guy I'd ever met.

"You two made a great team," I said. "I can just tell."

He nodded, and suddenly it seemed like the past was on him, weighing on his conscience in layers of memories. But he didn't seem overwhelmed, just peaceful. Our food arrived, and he dug in for a while in silence before putting down his knife and fork.

"Winnie was everything to me. We were from totally different backgrounds. My dad was a carpenter but died when I was small; his sister raised me. I didn't know my mom. We were poor. It took a lot of hard work for me to start my own business and a lot more work until it was the way I wanted. Sustainable, good for the planet, and high-quality. But Winnie..."

"Winnie..." he continued, "...was wealthy. The Locklows have more money than they know what to do with. And she trusted me to invest her money into the business. She was savvy, too. She knew how to make it happen. Because of her, we started getting wood from people who look after trees and forests. Because of her, we managed to cut emissions. The business is the way it is because she made it happen. I was just the brain, I guess. But she was the heart."

His words made my heart ache, but an ugly streak of jealousy ran through me too. I couldn't admit it to myself, but I would have given anything to trade places with Winnie, however short her life was just because of how happy she made Max.

As I let that thought sit uneasily between us, he looked up and nodded at me while staring over my shoulder. "Someone you know?"

I turned around and saw her. She'd been sitting at a booth in the corner, must have been since we came in. I couldn't fathom how I hadn't noticed her. My mother, Alice, got up and threw a dollar on the counter. I stood as she passed, wary and nervous.

"Sophie," she said, almost without a trace of expression. People used to say I would look like her when I grew up, which was uncomfortably true. My mother shared my athletic figure, though her arms were more muscular than mine, and three births had widened her hips a little. She was an inch shorter than me, but I felt myself wilt under her cold stare as she approached.

"Mom?" I said. I posed it as a question, knowing that the slightest hint of entitlement or presumption would provoke a quarrel. I didn't want that in front of Max.

"I wondered when I'd see you," my mom said. As she did, she drew a sharp breath as though somehow the sight of me was offensive to her. Her eyes moved to Max, then back at me. "How are you tonight, Mr. Fircress?" she said without even a trace of pretended enthusiasm.

"I'm just fine, Mrs. Gardner," replied Max. He read the room warily from his seat. "I was just taking Sophie out for dinner to say thank you."

"Really? I'm glad she's of some use to you," my mom said. She'd zipped up her coat. "I'd invite you over for dinner, Sophie, but I can see you're busy. Truth is, I haven't exactly missed you causing trouble out here."

"The feeling's mutual, mom," I said, almost under my breath. Her mere presence made me feel like a grounded teenager again, gritting my teeth and bracing myself for the inevitable lecture.

"Glad to hear it," said Alice. "After all, we wouldn't want any misunderstandings, would we?"

She turned and walked out of the door. I sat down and tried to pretend it didn't bother me, but Max could see it did, he could see how much I was hurting inside, and that was the worst thing of all.

Chapter 6

Max

On the porch that night, we stood together nearly an hour after we had come across Alice. Sophie withdrew into herself after that, offering one-word answers when I tried to get the conversation back on track and get her mind off meeting her mother that way. I could see how shaken up she was.

"Looks like things are pretty tough with your mom," I asked, thinking it best to just talk about it.

She nodded, looking a little miserable. I couldn't stand to see her look like that.

"It's been so long. I guess I just expected things to have changed between us. But..." She broke off, and I saw the beginnings of a tear gathering in her eyes.

"You know, it's not my place to say, but your mom..."

"...seems kind of cold?" said Sophie, laughing. "Try being raised by her. My ninth birthday present was a fifteen-mile hike, for God's sake." I smiled.

I was beginning to get the impression that Sophie's life hadn't been easy, but that made her all the more impressive.

So I did something unexpected, something I didn't even know I was going to do until it was done. I hugged Sophie and smelled the sweet softness of her hair as I pulled her close. I wanted to let her know that I cared for her and would do everything I could to help her. To my surprise, she didn't awkwardly recoil or pull away but let her head rest on my shoulder for a moment. It was the most comforting thing in the world.

We walked back inside and up the stairs, where she walked down the other way toward her room after thanking me again for the meal and for being there for her. I watched her go and only moved when I had the click of her key turning. I retired to my room after, her scent still lingering on my skin.

All night I lay awake, feeling the scar burn on my chest as the moon cast a soft, white light over my body. I longed for someone to hold me close as Winnie had, but as it crept towards morning, I shut my eyes for a few precious moments of sleep.

It seemed like I blinked and was opening my heavy eyes to start the day, only to be shocked at seeing Mindy standing in front of my open bedroom door.

"Sweetheart?" I said. I normally never had a visit from my daughter this early in the morning. As she peeked in and looked at me, I saw she was dressed for school.

Mindy didn't move but looked at me. She was waiting for me. I got out of bed and grabbed a robe. As I came towards the doorway, she held out her hand, and we walked down the stairs together.

Unbelievable, I thought.

It was like Mindy was coming back to herself, back to her old habits. We'd walked down the stairs together every morning when Winnie had been alive.

At the breakfast table, I saw Sophie, and we smiled at one another, one more of those secret, special smiles that had become our daily ritual. The smile meant *I like being here, I like being here with you, and I like you.*

Or so I hoped.

"Did you get her dressed this morning?" I asked, and Sophie shook her head.

"Miss Fiercress got herself organized this morning, didn't she?" said Sophie to Mindy, who smiled and nodded.

I shook my head, astonished at the closeness that had developed between them in just a few days. Sophie had been here less than a week, and she'd already made more progress with Mindy than I had in a few years. I did not doubt that I'd picked the right person for her, and it left me contemplative as I kissed Mindy on the head and watched Sophie pack her into Winnie's old Camero for the drive to school less than an hour later. Mindy took her sketchbook with her. It was already looking half-full with drawings, bright and sunny.

After watching them drive off, I retired to my desk and began to read company reports, but after a little while, my scar was burning, and my eyes were blearing from the glare of my computer screen. There was so much to do, and so many of the reports weren't making sense. From the way they were written, I would have expected our profit margins to be so much smaller, given that we'd decreased annual spending year on year since Winnie's death. And yet stocks were up, and orders were growing, and somehow, it was all being met. I had to hand it to my brother-in-law. Turns out he did have an eye for business after all.

As I left the house a few hours later, I saw Winston walking up the track toward the guesthouse. He looked a little ragged, his hair askew and dark circles under his eyes. I suspected he'd been drinking. Winston loved to drink, buy expensive wines, and show them off to his college buddies. I didn't mind it and occasionally indulged him with something nice for Christmas. But as we waved at one another and I watched his shadow, cast long from his lanky body in the morning light, I wondered why he hadn't spoken to me since he arrived. But I put it out of my mind, knowing as I did that I had something important to do today.

I was going to see Sophie's father.

As I was tossing and turning last night, I decided to go see Craig, hoping to find a way to smooth things over between Sophie and her family. She was doing so much for my own, and it only made sense to see how I could help her reconcile with her family.

Craig was a household name, a veteran of the airstrip with over thirty years and a record 50,000 hours of flight time. A record for Criker's Isle, that is, where most pilots only made the round trip to the mainland a few times a week. I'd met him once or twice before Winnie died, at a community barbeque and school events, where my stories about pine furniture to the kids were nothing compared to the anecdotes of his flying days. I knew he could be persuaded to let Sophie into the Gardner's lives.

The Gardner house was a bungalow, a mile or so up a road that led out of town and into the foothills of Mount Criker. From there, it was a few hours' short hike to the base of the peak or a longer, steadier climb leading to the mountain's south side. It was a popular spot for climbers and bouldering, which drew much-needed tourism and travel to the town in the Summer. The slopes looked dry and clear to me, and I promised myself I'd take Sophie up one of the cliff faces if she felt up to it.

At the top of the road was a small village, just a few houses on either side of the road. Most of them looked old and worn, but the Gardner residence looked well-maintained, with a few beds of flowers in the front yard and a fresh lick of paint on the porch. I parked my car on the driveway, climbed the porch steps, and rang the bell.

I knew Craig would be home as I had called up the airstrip while I watched Sophie and Mindy drive off, and he knew I knew because after I rang the bell a second time, the door opened quietly, and before me stood Sophie's dad, dressed in a polo shirt and pair of cargo pants.

"Mr. Gardner?" I said, mustering up all the politeness and decency I could. "Could I take a moment of your time?"

He peered out at me. "Max? Mr. Fircress?" He opened the door and gestured for me to come inside. "Please, call me Craig. My wife's not home," he said. "They're cleaning the resort today. Still a few guests up there, if you can believe it. Even with this weather we've been having."

"Glad to hear it, Craig," I said. As I entered the kitchen, I saw his flight jacket resting on a chair. Unhappiness tumbled in the air as I stood in the house, which had made Sophie who she was.

Just then, I recognized the dining table. It was a Fircress Furniture table, an early model. "Well, I'll be damned," I said.

He followed my gaze to the table and laughed nervously. "We bought that last year. Mighty fine piece of furniture. Reasonable price, too. Not like a lot of this eco-environmental stuff they're selling nowadays. I liked all the stuff you were telling the kids on Founder's Day. You remember the speech you did?"

That had been three years ago, the Summer before Winnie passed, but Craig was talking about it as though it had happened yesterday. I laughed meekly. "I think you might be the only one in the audience who was paying any attention. None of the kids did, that's for sure!"

He smiled and brushed my self-deprecation off. "Anyway, I said to myself, gotta get one of those tables. Alice isn't as fond of it as I am, but..." He broke off. "So, what can I do for you today,

Max? He looked at his watch. "Got a flight later," he added.

We both knew he wasn't too keen on me being there. It wasn't as though Craig's presence at the airfield was essential these days. He had Jake and Steve, two boys from town, who happily piloted and landed the planes. He poured me a cup of coffee and motioned for me to sit. He busied himself with a dish in the sink while I sat. I don't drink coffee, but it seemed rude to refuse.

"Well, sir, it's about Sophie, actually." I noticed him almost imperceptibly pause his task while he stood by the sink and then carried on.

"Oh, I see," he said and continued to fumble with the pot. "How's she doing? Things working out okay at, uh, Fairview?"

"Just fine, sir. She's doing a fantastic job. What I wanted to talk to you about was, well, Sophie's family situation. Not that it's any of my business, and I wouldn't have come, only…"

I had his full attention now. Craig turned around, and I heard a breath escape his lungs slowly. "Oh yeah?" he said, and the pain of years crossed his face like a shadow.

"The truth is…" I said slowly, "…I wonder if either you or Alice would like to come up to the house sometime. See Sophie, and meet Mindy. The two of them together, well. They're just wonderful, and it might—"

But he shook his head as I said the words, and it stopped me dead in my tracks.

"You have no right," he said quietly. "No right to come in here and ask me a thing like that. God, if Alice knew you were even here today, I'd never hear the end of it."

I froze. I'd blustered in so headstrong and confident, but when I saw the look in Craig's eyes, I felt like I'd made a terrible mistake.

I stood, pushing my coffee cup gently away from me. "I apologize, Mr. Gardner. I really do. You're correct, of course. I have no right. I just came because, well, because I'm fond of Sophie already. And I don't want her to be miserable when she could be very happy on Criker's Isle. Please forgive me." I turned and made ready to leave. I wanted to get out of the room, where the tension seemed drawn like a bowstring, and the air hung heavy with bad memories and hurt feelings. My chest was on fire.

"You want to know why Alice and Belinda don't like Sophie being here?" said Craig before I'd made my way out.

I turned and looked at him slowly.

Craig Gardner's lip curled a little, and then he answered his own question.

"Guilt."

I was about to say something in response, but he went on.

"Guilt is a powerful thing, Max. It ruins lives. It's ruined my life. Fourteen years I've waited for her to...to come home. And now she is here, and...guilt." As he said it, he threw his hands up in a gesture of futility.

"Sophie can forgive. I know she can."

Craig nodded. "That's my Sophie," he said quietly. His eyes misted a little as he said it. "Can we forgive ourselves, though?"

I looked at him. He looked ten years older than when we'd begun the conversation.

"Well, Mr. Gardner, when you have an answer to that, you let me know. In the meantime, I'm waiting at Fairview."

I stepped out of the house, leaving the old man alone with the ghosts. I headed straight home. Sophie and Mindy would be home in less than half an hour. As I rounded the corner in my jeep, I saw a police car in the driveway.

"Mother of Christ," I said to myself. "You creep."

But as I drove up, I saw Trevor standing at my door and relaxed.

"That's a fine cruiser," I said. He turned around to look at me and started to walk over quickly. "But I was worried you were someone else for a second."

Either Trevor didn't get the joke, or he was much too worried about something to laugh.

"Afternoon, Mr. Fircress," he said. "Can I talk to you inside for a second?"

Chapter 7

Sophie

"And I mean, last week! There were no tantrums, fighting, *nothing*," Mrs. Deleaney, Mindy's teacher, whispered conspiratorially on the phone. "You don't happen to have her on any new *medications* or anything, do you? Only, that's the kind of thing we ought to know, for—"

"I'm so glad to hear she's doing well," I said. "And no, there's no medication. I think she's turning a corner. Anyway, thanks, Ellen. We'll see you tomorrow."

I put the phone down. "Mindy!" I called.

She came running from behind the house, where we'd been looking at a toad together. I couldn't stand it, but Mindy had loved looking at the thing. Today she'd taken me for a walk towards the Northern cliffs. We passed the guesthouse, but there was no sign of Winston.

I gazed at her sadly as she ran into the house. I'd only been here for two weeks, but some part of me impatiently hoped that she might say something to me, just a word. We'd grown all but inseparable, to the point where Mindy would hold my hand and happily splash me with puddles. She even allowed me to help her do up her yellow raincoat, something which shocked Max when he saw me doing it.

"She won't even let me *touch* the thing," he said.

Sometimes I got the feeling he was insecure about how Mindy had responded to me, but I knew it was because of the distance between us, not the intimacy, and I had told him so.

"When she opens up to *you*..." I told him, "...that's how we'll know she's really making progress." I still saw myself as just a nanny to Mindy, even if my heart warmed when she looked at me or waved or managed to evade capture during hide-and-go-seek.

I believe in a lot of things that are old-fashioned in modern childcare. I still like to play classical music for kids. I don't think it makes them smarter, but I think any new sound is exciting for a child. Mindy never spoke, but she sure could yell when she was mad and hummed now and then. I'd caught her humming a fragment of a piece of Mozart I liked to play on Max's stereo while she drew and beamed with pride.

Of course, there were miles to go, and I knew she'd need to try again at therapy if she ever stood a chance of recovering. Max had opened up about how their attempts at therapy had been unsuccessful and how their last attempt had led to Mindy withdrawing even deeper. Her therapist had suggested giving Mindy time to get there on her own and tell us what she needed. The shock of Winnie's death had been delayed, a gradual process as the daily realization that her mother wasn't coming back had set in through weeks and months.

I longed for Max to be with us more, but he'd recused himself from our daily lives ever since the day after our disastrous meal at the diner. He was up early and walked long hours in his study. I saw him in the evenings, and we still ate together, just like a real family.

Not just like a real family, Sophie. You're not part of the family.

I tried to remain detached, but I couldn't. Mindy needed love, and I loved to give it. And in return, she noticed me and made me feel something I'd never felt before. Her mere toleration of my presence would have been enough, but her recognition made my maternal instincts soar. And Max, well.

I find it important to say things out loud, so the night after we ate and he embraced me in his strong, supple arms, I'd said the words into my pillow.

I have a crush on you. I said it so quietly that even I couldn't really hear the words.

Pathetic, I know.

But it was true.

I missed him when he was away, and when he wasn't, I longed to be closer to him. I cherished the memory of his embrace more than any memory I'd had with any boyfriend. We were friends, and I was his nanny. I knew that was how it was, and I knew that if I were to make my feelings known, it would be a greater betrayal of his and Mindy's trust than I could bear to inflict on them. So I busied myself with entertaining, teaching, educating, and making a haven for Mindy at Fairview as the nights began to draw in.

We came in by the front door. While Mindy put her things away and started to undo her laces, I stooped to pick up her sketchbook, which she'd left by the door. I opened it, looking at the new sketches happily. A few of them were of me, which brought a tinge of embarrassment to my cheeks. But at least as many of them were of her dad in one of his checkered plaid shirts or lying on a sofa. I smiled as I saw them, recognizing Max and realizing that Mindy had begun to notice her father. Outside, through the open door, I watched the sun climb out through a patch of cloud and heard a car engine in the distance.

I turned the page of the book and saw a sketch I didn't like. This one showed a tall, thin stick man with a scruffy mess of hair, and next to him, a female figure lying over. Mindy had drawn a thick pair of tears dropping from her eyes with a blue crayon.

"Mindy?" I called. "Would you come here for a second?"

She willingly obeyed, happily bounding up to my side.

"Who is that, Mindy? Who's the tall man?" I was trained to spot a child afraid of an adult, and any adult who was the object of fear was often drawn as being impossibly tall or scary in a child's drawing. And what frightened me the most was that Mindy had labeled the drawing with a W and I.

"W and I..." I said. "What does that mean, Mindy? Who's the tall man?"

She looked at her wellington boots and didn't say anything.

"Is it someone around here?" I said.

She nodded.

"Is it Winston?"

She nodded again.

"And who's this, on the floor here? She looks sad, doesn't she?" Mindy nodded. Very sad.

Could Winston have hurt Mindy?

I took a deep breath. I didn't want to push her. "Is it you, honey?"

She sighed and stamped her foot. I could tell I'd made her mad.

"Who is Winston with?" I said. "She looks sad, Mindy. I just want to know."

Mindy looked up at me, deep into my eyes. I thought she might be about to speak, but I heard a low moan in her voice.

"Is it mommy?" I said, at last. A deafeningly loud silence passed between us.

That's when Mindy bolted through the open door.

Oh no. What have I done?

I followed her out, half-tripping on the porch as I did. Mindy was running down the slope to the foot of the driveway. I ran after her, but she wanted to get away, get away from whatever I'd made her think, and to her, I was the cause of it, the anguish that made her run. She stopped dead center in the middle of the grass, and I ran up to her.

"Well, isn't that a nice thing to see?"

I rose gently, keeping Mindy pressed to my side so she couldn't see him. I didn't need to turn to see who it was.

"What do you want, Derrick?" I said slowly and carefully.

He was standing at the foot of the driveway, close to where my sister had been. He'd planted his feet just over the other side. He wasn't even standing on Max's property. He'd tanned a little and was bigger than the last time I saw him. Not skinny or weak now, but grown up. A little fat around the waist. A rough stubble had grown over his face, and his hair, once scraggly and unkempt, was meticulously slicked with wax. But those beady little eyes were just the same as they always had been—accusing, glinting, searching for any weakness wherever they turned.

"Just came by to see how my Sophie's getting on," he said. "How are you up here?"

I said nothing. "Go inside," I whispered to Mindy. "Go inside and shut the door."

She obeyed, running past me where the air had thickened with fear. I didn't say anything until I heard the door close.

"I'm getting on just fine, Derrick."

He looked around scornfully at the trees and high hedges around Fairview. "Must get awful lonely up here," he said. "Don't you ever feel like coming into town?"

My hands balled into fists, and I stood, stock still, ready to back away should he take a single step toward me. I was wondering if my phone was in my pocket. But who would I call if it was?

He motioned towards the house with his hat. "See you got that wild child tamed a little. Good to see that. Hey, is it true she bites?"

I shook my head. I was glad he was standing fifty feet away, so he couldn't see my lip trembling a little. What frightened me most wasn't Derrick but the way I felt now. I felt that fear rise through my stomach and clasp its hands around my shoulders, ready to throw me. I felt like I'd never left that dingy apartment on the mainland where we'd lived, that fear of what he'd say when he found out I hadn't made him dinner, washed his clothes, or given him every last damn cent I had.

"Well, Sophie, you don't say much these days, do you? Guess that girl isn't the only wild thing that's been tamed..."

I spat right on the ground. "Don't you mention her to me, Derrick. Don't you speak her name or come close to her."

He just laughed when I said that, like I was joking. I hated it when he did that. "Oh, Sophie," he said, laughing. "My Sophie."

"*I am not your Sophie*," I said through gritted teeth.

"I see that," said Derrick. "I see it. I should have known someone like you didn't believe in second chances."

"After what you did?" I said. "No. I don't think I do."

"And what's that? Take you away from Criker's Isle? Give you a new life?"

I sneered. He was delusional. He'd given me nothing but heartache and fear. And the son of a bitch didn't even realize it.

"You can just get out of here, *Sheriff*," I said.

"Sure, sure," said Derrick. "I can see when I'm not wanted," he added bitterly.

He turned to go, and I relaxed, just for a moment. But I tensed up again when he next spoke.

"You ever change your mind, though, I'll be happy to show you round town sometime. Heck..." he said, scratching his head and replacing his hat, "...we could go see a movie. Get all romantic like old times."

"Fat chance," I growled after him as he entered his cruiser and drove off, a smug smile on his face.

I watched his cruiser until it wasn't in view before heading back up the house. When I got to the front, Mindy was at the door. I shook my head and walked towards her. "We're going to play inside for the rest of the day," I said to her.

Chapter 8

Max

Every day for a week since Trevor told me he thought my wife might have been murdered, I woke up in agony. The wound, which had long closed, still burned from where it had hurt my insides. After a week of hiding it from Sophie, suffering in silence, I wised up. Winnie's voice rang in my ears: *a boy thinks he can solve a problem on his own. A man takes help whenever he can get it.*

So I called my doctor in the morning. "Hey, doc," I said. "Been a while."

"Max? Is that you? How are you, son?"

"Not so good. It's back, the pain, I mean."

"Well, I'm sorry to hear that, Max. Did you follow my advice?"

"Well, I'm eating better. And I'm doing okay, I guess. Happy. Like we talked about."

"Glad to hear it, son. And exercise?"

"I walk a little, I guess."

"Walking's no good for this, Max. That gash went right

through your abdominal muscles. Half of the damage was internal. That's where the pain starts from, doesn't it? And finishes up in your chest?"

"That's right."

"Do something for me, will you? Is the weather bad out there on Criker's Isle right now?"

"Not so bad. I mean, Summer's over, but the weather's held a few days now. Maybe a week."

"Well, sounds like you might still have a chance to climb if you like. Take a friend, and make a day of it. I promise you, laying around is not going to put an end to this."

"Right, doc."

"If only they were all like you, Max."

He put the phone down, and I thought of Sophie.

I couldn't deny that I'd been missing her in my life. Her quiet presence at my dinner table made life seem brighter. And I'd longed for her since I'd held her on the porch, smelled her and felt her soft hands on me, and looked into her green eyes, full of hope. There was something heady and delightful in watching her and Mindy, which made my heart race and my thoughts clear.

It was clear I wanted more than mere friendship with her. But I couldn't. I knew I couldn't.

For years I'd believed I would always be alone, and now that belief had grown around me, like a vine through the house, through the grounds of Fairview and all the fabric of my life, strangling anything that might take root. I was bitter. And besides, I was almost a decade older than Sophie. No way a beautiful woman like her would feel the same way about me, a broken widower.

Nevertheless, the pain sharpened my nerves and focused me. As I entered my study and sat at my desk, I set out to untangle the mess of reports and files, with hard copies lying strewn across my desk. I put on a pair of reading glasses and hopped straight to it.

I started by circling every purchase order on our books. So far, so good. Then, I marked the invoices in a copy of the database. Once I pulled them up, I noticed what had been bothering me.

The number of materials we'd bought did not equal what we'd been billed. In fact, it vastly outnumbered it. Our budget for timber was almost a third of what we'd acquired. And yet, we weren't in the red anywhere.

Secondly, we were cutting costs in manufacturing but not in labor. That was bizarre. Again, I tracked the spending cuts for the last four quarters. "Winston, Winston, Winston," I said to myself. "What have we got here?"

First, our business rates were getting smaller for the first three quarters. That was odd. Had we sold off any sites? No. So, why were we manufacturing on a smaller scale? Storage. Storage must be the answer. And it explained why we weren't increasing hires but increasing production. Employees were working faster because the materials were on site. But what were we stockpiling? And why, when our material was coming from renewable sources? Sure, it saved on transportation, and I liked the idea of that, but if that was the case, why weren't we shipping in bigger batches? It all needed answering, and, fortunately, I knew just who to speak to about it.

I stood and left the house. I walked up the hill, and at the top, I turned around. Fairtown was visible in the midday sun. Ahead of me lay the port, and to the south, the school, hidden under the shadow of the hill below the airstrip. Mindy would be there right now, I expected. I wondered what time Sophie would be back.

By the time I reached the guesthouse, I noticed he was already gone. Winston's rental car was missing. I took the spare key from my pocket and knocked on the door. No answer. Had he really left without saying goodbye?

Inside, the place was immaculate. The usually scruffy Winston had tidied it very well. The bed was made. And his office was sparkling. He'd even put away the usual detritus—files, boxes of papers, and so on—in the filing cabinet. I called him from my cell phone.

"How are you, old sport?" a voice said. It sounded out of breath.

"Winston?" I said. "Everything alright?"

"Just fine! I'm on the mainland. I was called back...running for a train right now, actually; I'll be back next week, though, if that's alright. Say, can I call you back later?"

I sighed and rolled my eyes. "Sure thing, Winston. You call me back."

We'd had a few short meetings during his time here, less than I had hoped. And now he'd just up and left?

As I put the phone down, I rolled my eyes. My brother-in-law was a scatterbrain, always has been. I knew perfectly well who would be calling the other back later.

As I ascended the hill the short distance to the house, I saw the car Sophie was using parked in the driveway, and my heart whispered, *just the two of you together, now.* It was a guilty, secret thought, and I knew nothing would come of it. But I knew the cloud that had come over me in the last week would clear when I saw Sophie, though I couldn't admit why.

As I entered, I saw her leafing through a magazine at the kitchen table. I could see from how her slim shoulders were locked straight as she read that she was worried about something.

"Would you like some coffee?" I asked.

She looked up, anxious, and her harried, tired eyes met mine. I could see she'd slept as poorly as I had.

"I'm fine," she said. I could hear the tremble in her voice. Something wasn't right; that much was clear. "Guess I'm a little jittery today."

Part of me wanted to ask her what was wrong, what could have made the strong, bright soul in front of me overcast with anxiety. But I knew not to pry, that whatever she had to tell me, she would tell me when she was ready. So I sat by her and opened a catalog I'd been sent. It contained information on a new line of products, the first that Winston had supervised. As I looked at the bright, glossy pages, I became aware of the stillness that had settled over the kitchen.

After a little while, I looked up and noticed Sophie's eyes had moistened with tears. I opened my mouth to speak, but she shook her head.

"I just...I..." she said, and then began to cry, with her head in her hands.

"Sophie?" I said. "What's wrong?" Concern and fear rose in me, and I stood up from the table, moving around to her side. As she stifled her sobs, I put a hand on her shoulder, and she looked up at me. That glimmer of hope, again. "We're friends, aren't we, Sophie?" I said.

She nodded and smiled through the tears which ran down her cheeks. "It's Derrick," she said, eventually.

A cold vein of anger rose in my gut. "What did he do?" I asked quietly.

"He was at the house yesterday," she said. "He was standing in the driveway. Oh, Max, Max, he's just...I'll never get free of him, will I?"

I looked at her face, her proud, solemn face. I knew then that Derrick must have hurt her in some way, done something to her when they were young. "You'd better tell me about it," I said.

An hour later, we sat together in silence on the sofa. I'd been angry at first, then my anger had given way, useless as it was, and I'd been bent on comforting her. She'd told me of her life with Derrick, how they'd escaped to the mainland. His controlling behavior, the fight between them. Her flight to freedom, everything. I'd said little and asked a few questions here and there. My respect for Trevor had grown a great deal when she told me how he helped her escape. It made me trust him all the more.

"You're so good with Mindy," I said. "Not just Mindy," I added. "Me too."

She looked at me, brightness returning to her wide, soulful green eyes. "That's all I want," she said. "Not anything to do with Derrick or my folks. I don't want to deal with any of it, Max. I just want to be here. Here...with you."

She put her head on my shoulder, and I put an arm around her. For someone who's in pain most days, I felt rawer, more tender at that moment than I had in a long time. It was like the darkness of the years faded in her presence, the light she cast around my life thawing the parts of me that had grown cold and stiff. I'd thought a part of me was dead, too, after Winnie passed away.

Now I realized that Sophie had brought that part back to life, unfrozen it from its long, forgetful sleep.

An errant strand of hair had come loose from her ponytail and fallen over her face. I brushed it behind her ear, and the warmth from her temple sent a shiver of longing through me.

"Aren't we a pair?" I said. "We both think we'll never be free of the past."

She turned at that and sat up, looking into my eyes. It was like I could hide nothing of myself from her, and despite all the emotions whirling in the air and settling heavily over the rooms of Fairview, I wished I could kiss her, there and then.

"But together..." she said, "...together I feel like we could be. And I feel like Mindy could be too."

The thought of my daughter being happy again, drawing again, feeling the sun on her face, and beginning to stir back into life lit a fire in my chest. Once a wide, empty mausoleum, Fairview seemed like the coziest, safest place on earth.

"Whatever happens, Sophie, you'll always be safe here," I said. I meant it and knew even then that I would do anything to make that happen.

Chapter 9

Sophie

A few days later, I woke at dawn, with the birds chittering away in the dark, and watched the mist receding through the hedges at Fairview. It was a restlessness that stirred me from sleep. I was vigilant after seeing Derrick days ago and nervous at the tender moment Max and I had shared in the living room yesterday. My mind was a mass of emotions, turbulent and unpredictable, like the ocean surrounding Criker's Isle. As a teenager, I'd watched the sea and thought it was romantic. Now I knew the truth—that its restlessness was unpleasant and stressful, and to feel like that was to be robbed of sleep, left feeling tired and drained.

I went to the kitchen and brewed a pot of coffee before straightening out some of Mindy's things. I picked up the sketchbook from its place by the front door and stepped out to look at the view as the sunlight began to sail across the hilltops and illuminate the house. It was going to be a beautiful day, and the chill had already left the air as I stood on the doorstep, looking at Mindy's sketchbook.

Had she drawn a memory or merely imagined it?

The picture seemed to show Winston hurting Winnie in some way, making her cry. There was no doubt about it. Mindy seemed to perceive some threat between the two.

I'd disliked Winston from the moment I saw him, and his sudden departure without saying goodbye to Max hadn't done much to endear me to the tall, skinny man with the scrappy hairdo. I'd even watched the guesthouse from my bedroom window for a few nights, wondering what he might be doing up there so late at night. But none of it was enough to suggest Winston might have been cruel to Winnie—or to Mindy. By all accounts, according to Max, he was a stand-up guy. Perhaps it was just that he reminded Mindy of her mother, and that made him someone to be feared. It was clear the memories of Mindy's separation from her mother were a shadow on her. To avoid dealing with things, she had buried all the parts of herself, including her speech. I couldn't blame her.

I went into her room and woke her at 6:30, brushing her cheek as she slept quietly. I was happy to see Mindy had been persuaded not to suck her thumb, and as she woke gently, her eyes darted to meet mine. She sat in bed and threw her hands onto her lap, smiling at me.

"Good morning, beautiful," I said. "How did you sleep?"

Mindy nodded. We'd managed to get a few nods or shakes of her head from her over the last week. I was thrilled to see her communicating. It sparked an idea in my head, and I took a pad of paper and a pen from her desk as she gently eased herself out of bed and stretched, tugging at the hem of her pajama top. It had a pink dinosaur on the front.

"What do you want for breakfast today, Min?" I said. I offered her the pad and pen.

She looked suspiciously at me. I knew she thought this was an attempt to get her to speak, but I had to be gentle and make sure she knew I didn't expect more than she could give.

She took the pad and pen and sat back down on the bed. After a while, she scribbled something on the pad and gave it back to me. She kept drawing a circle in the air with the pen while I beamed at the words written on the paper in front of me.

Eggs, please.

"Eggs it is," I said, trying to stop myself from laughing and punching the air. "Now, let's get you dressed!"

I put the paper in front of Max at the breakfast table. Before grinning at me, he studied it like it was one of his technical manuals or business sheets. There was so much gratitude in that smile that I couldn't hold his gaze for long.

Before we left, Max asked to speak with me.

"You're a star," he said, and I felt pride and happiness bloom inside me. I reached out to put a hand on his arm but thought better of it in front of his daughter. "I wanted to ask you something."

"What's that?" I said.

"Ever been rock climbing?" he said.

"As in...climbing, climbing? Scaling walls, finding footholds? Just a rope between you and a grisly death? Never in my life." My mom, who worked at the tourist resort in the Summer, had tried a hundred times to get me to go climbing. I hadn't really been interested.

He laughed. "It's nothing like that. Anyway, pretty soon, the weather will be too unstable on Criker to go. But I wanted to take you. Give you a taste of what you're in for next summer. How's that sound?"

I didn't know what to say. The idea of spending a day with Max filled me with happiness. But the idea of dangling on a cliff edge...that made me feel all kinds of nervous.

It didn't get lost on me his assumption that I'd be here in a year...as if he was making future plans that included me.

At the risk of letting my mind spiral, I turned my full focus back to the present. I looked at him nervously, half-wanting to refuse.

"I promise..." he said, "...you'll be completely safe. After you've dropped Mindy at school, meet me by the Mount Criker's trail. There's a place I know."

He patted me encouragingly on the shoulder and walked off, rolling his shoulders and barely looking his thirty-eight years. I looked down, thankful I was wearing my cargo pants.

***

After I dropped Mindy off at school, I drove back. But instead of going through town, I took a right, turning up the old mining track. I guessed the house where my parents lived was just over the hill, but I put that out of my mind and carried on up the slopes of Mount Criker. The high peak was barely visible, still wrapped in the morning mist, but as the road climbed, it became overcanopied by dense forest. I was heading northeast now until I saw a sign for the hiking trail, and nearby, Max's jeep was parked on the side of the road in a shallow gulf.

I stopped and pulled in before I saw Max waving at me from the other side of the parking lot. He was dressed in a windbreaker and a pair of cargo pants, looking rugged and handsome. He had a set of neatly coiled ropes on the ground. Nearby, on a sheet of cloth, there was a selection of devices, pulleys, clips, sandbags, and carabiners. The kind of stuff you'd have if you were an experienced climber about to attempt a serious rock face. Not the sort of stuff you'd need if you'd never been climbing in your life.

"What's all that stuff for?" I said as I got out of the car. I'd expected a light scramble up a hilltop, not a full-scale assault.

"All to keep you safe, of course," he said, packing his things into a pair of cloth bags. "Here, put these on," he said, tossing me a harness and a helmet. The helmet felt strong and sturdy, but the harness was barely more than a few strips of cloth. "Are you sure this is a good idea?" I said, scrambling after him as he started making down a track that ran from the parking lot into the woods.

"It's perfectly safe, Sophie. We're going to do a little rock face today. The route's been marked out before by experienced climbers. Actually, it's the cliff I learned to climb on when Winnie and I first came out here."

"The *cliff*?" I replied.

When we got to the place, I looked up. It wasn't very high, maybe thirty feet or a little more. But to someone who had no idea how to climb, it wasn't exactly a walk in the park.

"See the cams?" Max said, pointing up to the rock. I followed his fingers, noticing how close he was standing to me. His presence was reassuring.

"I already put them in while you were dropping off Mindy. They're anchor points, see? At every stage, I'll clip you in, and there's a guide rope here..." Max pointed to a thin pair of ropes running down from the cliff face at the bottom, "...which will hold you the whole way. I could belay you, but I thought you might prefer me to come up with you the first time."

I was feeling pretty anxious, but I put on the shoes Max had brought for me and donned the harness, slipping my legs into its loops and belting it around my waist. I felt a tinge of guilt as I realized the harness might have belonged to Winnie. Max helped me get my helmet on and clipped me in.

"You okay with this, Sophie?" he said, clipping the helmet in place. I felt a little embarrassed as he kneeled and put his hands around my legs, tightening the straps of my harness. He stood up. "You know, we don't have to do this if you don't want to. I just thought it might be fun. And you're perfectly safe. I promise."

I looked into his eyes and saw all kinds of unanswered questions in them. Did I feel safe with him? Did I want to be there? Did I want to spend time with him?

I resolved to be brave and try something new for once. All my life, I've taken the safest, easiest option. "Just remember I'm a beginner," I mumbled. This time, it wasn't embarrassment making me shy, but something else I'd felt as he fussed over my equipment.

We started by getting acquainted with the gear. Max listed everything we'd be using and explained what it was all for, clipping various metal devices onto my harness and having me practice with a few footholds. Within no time, I was shimmying up and down the first few feet of the rock face, sidestepping, learning to move, one limb at a time. It wasn't the death-defying sport I'd first imagined. Climbing was slow, methodical, about being prepared for everything, so there were never any mistakes—and even if there were, you had plenty of ways of getting out of a sticky situation.

Once we'd started to make our first climb together, I realized that even if I fell, the rope would catch me. It was secured into the various anchor points, and we often stopped so Max could clip me in. But it still started to feel intimidating after I'd managed to get myself ten feet off the ground. Behind me, the ground sloped away to the hiking trail, making it seem like we were higher up than we really were.

By the time we were twenty feet up, I was starting to feel a little out of my depth. It must have taken me thirty minutes or so to get that high, and my arms and legs already felt exhausted. "Up to you," said Max. "We can push on or descend now and take a break." But a rush of adrenaline was coursing through me, and I felt determined to push on and get to the top. I guess I wanted to impress Max.

My confidence grew as we climbed further and further, and I was clipped into more and more of the anchor points. "You're really good at this!" said Max. I was a little out of breath but exhilarated.

"I can't believe it," I said, in between taking deep breaths to steady my nerves. "We're almost there."

I was almost parallel with Max and could see there were just a few feet left to go. My left foot found a hold, then my right. Then my right hand found a crevice in the rock. I jammed my hand in, just the way Max had shown me. Then, my left hand searched for another hold. But the rock in front of me just looked flat. I was a little too far to the left of the route to find anything to grasp.

Props to you, I guess, mom. This isn't as easy as it seems.

"Get your left hand in with your right," said Max gently. He was hanging from the cliffside, casual as could be, watching me find my way.

"Okay," I said, a little flustered. I put my hands together.

"Now, find somewhere else for your right hand, then think about your feet," said Max.

I didn't listen, of course. It felt odd to make the stretch across the right into Max's space. So I moved my foot instead. But I was clinging too tightly with both hands to look down. I was climbing blind—something that Max had warned me not to do. My foot slipped, and as it did, my hands scraped free of the crevice in the rock. I was in freefall.

But Max caught me long before the rope did. Quick as could be, his hand reached out from its hold and grabbed my arm. He lifted me a little by my elbow, taking care not to pull on my arm and potentially dislocate it. He lifted me to his side, and as my hands found their footing, he said, "I've got you."

And as he said that, he leaned over and kissed me.

I've never felt anything like it, and the world swam before me as I held on for dear life. Why? What did it mean? I questioned it, but eventually, my brain gave up, and in the middle of adrenaline, safety, and the utter peace Max had brought to my life, I kissed him back.

We kissed for what seemed like the longest time before we broke off. I could see a trickle of sweat running down Max's temple, but he'd lifted me like I weighed nothing at all.

"Come on," he said, leaping the last few feet and pulling himself up onto the top of the cliff. "I'll hoist you up."

He kept himself anchored, swung his feet over the ledge, and reached down with his hand. I made a few cursory foot movements to get myself a little higher, and before I knew it, he'd pulled me up, over the ledge, and straight into his arms. I tore off my helmet and kissed him again as the sunlight coursed over our bodies, warm and beating as the valley stretched out before us.

Chapter 10

Max

I couldn't think of anything as we lay there in the grass, holding one another. Our kiss was like something passed between us. First, I led, holding Sophie, kissing her mouth, then her cheeks, and her neck. Then it would pass to her, and I let her climb into my lap as her legs wrapped around me. We'd ditched our gear for the time being and made our way to a grassy knoll. The sun was high in the sky, and the ground soft and warm as she made her first tentative explorations of my body.

In the glade, she unbuttoned my shirt and dropped low to my chest. Her hair had come loose from the tight bun she'd put it in to climb, and now her lips worked their way over my collarbone and neck while her hair hung soft and loose, electric on my skin. She ran a hand down to my belt, and I felt her palm press gently on the inside of my leg. I was hard for her, and she knew it.

"It's...it's been a long time," said Sophie, suddenly blushing.

I met her gaze as her lovely green eyes glinted in the bright sun. "For me too. We'll go as slow as you like," I said.

"Okay," Sophie said. "But, I want you," she whispered, and I shuddered with delight as I felt her hands unzip my pants while her mouth met mine again, and my heart leaped with joy at our union.

Before I knew it, she'd taken off my pants, and her left hand was cradling my hard cock. It felt enormous in her small hand, those delicate hands. How long I'd lingered over them, secretly wondering what they might do if we found ourselves alone?

Sophie stroked me to a full erection before lowering her mouth. I sat up a little, lovingly stroking her cheek with my hand before I felt her lips close around my shaft. With tiny, loving licks on the glans, she began to move her head up and down. As she did, I felt the shadows of my life fall away, felt everything fall away, and felt at one with her while she patiently sucked, moving her tongue in circles which made me shiver with pleasure.

She made a little moan as she moved her head up and down, more enthusiastically now. I felt myself begin to groan with pleasure, the noise starting deep from within my chest and traveling up until I was saying her name, "Sophie, Sophie," while she lovingly and tenderly offered herself to me.

Suddenly, I heard voices coming through the woods one by one. Sophie raised her head, wiping her lips. I was erect and pulsing in front of her. I'd been moments away from climaxing. Groaning, I reached for my pants and pulled them back on while Sophie sat beside me, laughing. It wasn't awkward, but whoever else was on the trail that morning had certainly killed the mood. We kissed and rose together as I grabbed my gear. I felt her take my hand in hers, and she whispered in my ear, "Can we stay out here today?"

We both beamed like a couple of teenagers as we gathered our things. After we'd walked around the rock face and back to the car, Sophie's eyes lit up as I pulled a picnic hamper from the bag.

"How did you...I swear..." she said, "...you are the most perfect man I've ever met."

That nagging voice spoke inside of me once more.

If you were perfect, would you have let her go down on you while your daughter was away at school?

I put it aside, doing my best not to be shadowed by guilt. In the sunlight, Sophie looked more beautiful than ever, a little sweaty from the climb and more than a little flushed from what we'd been doing at the cliff. I could tell by how she crossed and uncrossed her legs as we stood by the car that her panties were soaked through.

We walked on as I carried the hamper. "Do you suppose that's anyone we know?" said Sophie, gesturing to the voices which rang out further up the trail.

"Lord, I hope not," I replied, and we laughed again.

We stopped by a cliff edge further up the trail, one which looked out across the forest and gave a breathtaking view of Fairtown and the rolling, green hills which rose above it. From here, you could see the pine forest, the airstrip to the south, and Fairview, which was visible a few miles West on the island's edge.

"This is beautiful," said Sophie, and we stopped. I'd made us a sandwich with tomatoes and some mozzarella I'd found in the fridge that morning, and we ate happily in silence, unwilling to confront the fact that just an hour earlier, we'd been fully ready to make love there on top of the rock face we'd climbed. I wondered what that meant for the future.

"I used to think this place was unfinished," said Sophie after we'd finished lunch. "Like, I hadn't completed it. That's why I wanted to come back. But now I realize it's not the place. It's me that's unfinished. I'm like a story without an ending, Max."

I put a hand on hers as we sat on the blanket I'd spread. The sun had passed behind a cloud now, and there was a little chill in the air.

"There's nothing unfinished about you, Sophie. You've got your whole life ahead of you. Even though there might be things inside you that you still don't understand, me and Mindy are here for you. I want to help you. I just want you to be happy, I guess. And so does she."

As we both looked at the sea, crashing and violent in the distance, I felt a sigh escape Sophie. I knew she wouldn't be truly happy until Derrick was out of her life for good. I had a few things to say to him the next time we ran into one another.

"And I want you to be happy, Max. You're a wonderful father to Mindy. I know I'm...I mean, I know I can't be everything to Mindy." I knew exactly what she meant, and a tinge of sadness ran through me. Sophie would never be Mindy's real mother, even if the bond between them grew even stronger than it already was. Even if I wanted her close to me, forever, the way I'd thought I wanted Winnie.

"We'd better go," I said. "Mindy will be finishing school in an hour."

"Do you like ice cream?" said Sophie, and I laughed. I knew exactly what she was thinking.

***

At the school gates, Mindy beamed when she saw the two of us together. I hugged her, and she practically ran into my arms. Less than a month ago, it had been like she didn't even know I was there. But now, we stood together on the pavement, contented to be reunited with each other again. I beckoned Sophie towards me from the car, and she came over, fussing over Mindy and helping her with one of her bags and the sketchbook.

"How are you doing today, Min?" I asked her, and she nodded. "Good day?"

"Got much homework?" asked Sophie, and Mindy shook her head. "That's good news! How would you like it if your dad and I took you for some ice cream?"

Mindy nodded even more enthusiastically. Mindy loved to go for ice cream, and it was a great treat for her at the end of her two days at school. I looked at Sophie, and she looked at me, and we both laughed.

"Hey, Min," I said. "I think you really like Miss Gardner. Am I right about that?"

Mindy shyly clasped her arms together and nodded, this time slowly and bashfully. Sophie laughed and replied, "Well, that's good because I like you too." Mindy left my arms and hugged Sophie's leg. Sophie didn't know where to look and giggled while gingerly patting Mindy on the head. I could tell she was moved by Mindy's feelings for her.

"Ain't that adorable?" said a familiar voice behind us. "You guys just look like one big happy family right now."

I turned around and sighed, gritting my teeth in a gesture of politeness. "Hey, Belinda. You here for something?"

She didn't even look at me, not wanting to see the look of disdain in my eyes. I gave Sophie a reassuring glance.

It's alright. I'm here.

Belinda peered at Mindy, who was clinging to Sophie's leg. Her hands were thrust into the pockets of her coat. A cold breeze was starting to blow in from the harbor.

"I came by to pick up Joe Hanny's kid," she said, looking past the school and toward the sea. "He's off-island right now, working at the boatyard. Say, Min? How are you doing?"

Mindy said nothing. Whenever Belinda and I ran into one another at school, she always insisted on talking to Mindy. I snarled defensively, then checked myself. Mindy didn't need some stranger bothering her, but she also didn't need to see Belinda and me fighting. I glanced around nervously, looking to see if that familiar cop car was nearby.

"What do you want, Belinda?" Sophie asked.

Belinda took another step forward, ignoring her sister. "Mindy? I asked you something, sweetheart. Ain't you gonna talk to me?"

Mindy hid her head behind Sophie's leg. She obviously didn't want to engage with Belinda. As a matter of fact, none of us did.

Sophie's sister lifted her head and sneered at me. "A bit rude of her, don't you think, Max?" I could see the rage in her eyes. "I can see my sister's already working her magic," she said, stalking past us into the playground.

"Come on," I said. "Let's get to the car." Mindy ran right ahead, but Sophie just stood, silently looking back at her sister. Her face was closed to me now.

Chapter 11

Sophie

The weekend was a long, lonely one. I took Mindy out for walks and watched her draw. I felt desperate to stay close to her after Belinda's interruption at the schoolyard. At nights, after she'd gone to bed, I stayed up, but Max and I didn't talk much. We didn't know what to say to each other.

I wanted to feel his touch again, his kiss, pleasure him again like that day when we'd gone out climbing together. And yet, some part of me was determined not to push him to say anything about that day to me. Had it been a mistake? I wasn't sure. Max was still grieving for Winnie. I could tell that much. Maybe he felt guilty about approaching me again, especially while his daughter was in the house, a silent witness to the feelings that had grown between us.

He was mercifully preoccupied with his work, looking up errors and inaccuracies in financial reports from his company. And Mindy needed me; she'd been shaken up by seeing Belinda. I dreaded the PTA meeting on Monday when we'd have to be in the same room in front of Mindy's teachers and the other parents at the school.

Monday came, a cloudy, wintery day with a bank of fog setting over the shore, swooping up the hills to enclose Fairview. Mindy didn't feel like going outside, so I watched her playing in the house. She found a cute yellow bear and spent a little time running back and forth around Max's couch, making the bear pop up, give a wave now and then, and disappear. It made me laugh. Funny how easy it is for kids to make you laugh, even when the rest of life makes you gloomy. Thoughts of Derrick and Belinda were easily forgotten when she made her way onto my lap and sat there for a little while, pressing her head into my shoulder as though looking for a safe place to be.

"Having fun, you guys?" Max said when he came into the living room in the afternoon. He saw Mindy nestled next to me with one of her books and smiled at me. I smiled back, a longing smile full of unspoken want.

"I guess we'd better get going soon," said Max, brushing dust off his suit jacket. I thought it was adorable that he'd put a tie on to go to the school. I know he didn't like to dress up smart; he felt it was pretentious and silly. But he still looked handsome as he did up his cuffs, and seeing him adjust the belt on his trousers brought all kinds of forbidden images to my mind.

We drove to the school and arrived at 5:00 pm. I got Mindy out of the car while Max found a place to park, smartening her up. We'd put her in a pretty brown dress, a special-occasion dress with a white ribbon around the collar. Max and I knew the teachers would have good things to say, and we wanted to take Mindy out for dinner afterward. I took one of Mindy's hands, and Max took the other. A little nervous, we went inside.

In Mindy's classroom, there was an exhibit of folding boards of all the kids' drawings. Most of the kids had contributed three or four pictures and were busy telling their proud parents who stood behind them, smiling and nodding, while the little ones enumerated exactly which one of grandpa's dogs was in this one or what family vacation was depicted in bright, colorful crayon for all to see.

"I think before we talk, you'd better see what Mindy's drawn for us all," said Mrs. Deleaney. She was excited, and Max's jaw dropped as we progressed to the end of the display.

Like I said, most of the kids had drawn three or four pictures. Not Mindy, though. She'd filled an entire board by herself. There must have been ten or so of the images drawn on A3 paper with a variety of pens and colored pencils. And they were good, too, showing her and me in fields, relaxing together in the study, or eating breakfast together at the dinner table in Max's house. I was in almost all of them and blushed a little to see myself, cartoonish and illuminated in radiant, orange-colored pencil.

"It's pretty clear she's been under a good influence lately," said Mrs. Deleaney, laughing. "I haven't seen her so happy in a long time. But it's more than that. She plays with the other kids now, doesn't have tantrums..." She stopped and turned to Max, beaming. "You're very lucky to have her around."

I mostly just looked at my shoes while Max accepted the praise on my behalf. "I sure am, Mrs. D.," he said, resting a hand gently and inoffensively on my shoulder. "You have no idea."

It was like the gray skies parted when he said that.

"How are her grades coming along?" I said.

"Well, I'm pleased to say we actually have some *finished tests* this time," replied Mrs. Deleaney. "The big surprise for me is how well she's doing in literacy. You'd think that after so long..." she said, pausing, not wanting to mention Mindy's mutism, "...but no. Her reading and spelling have actually improved. Don't ask me how."

I had an answer for that. "Well, mutism doesn't necessarily

affect written spelling and literacy unless there's some underlying factor combining the two. In Mindy's case, I'm not surprised. Reading has been an escape for her. She reads a couple of books a week, which is exceptional for a kid her age."

"Well, goodness me!" replied Mrs. Deleaney. "I can see we have a very talented educator on our hands, as well as an excellent nanny. If you ever get bored of looking after just one kid, Sophie..." she said, giving Max and me a mock-conspiratorial look, "...I have sixteen more right here who could do with some persuading to read."

I groaned a little but accepted the compliment with grace. Mindy was tugging at my sleeve and pointing to me in the pictures.

"Thank you so much for your time, Mrs. D.," said Max. "I think Mindy's earned herself a real treat later. Don't you?"

We stood around for another hour or so before it was time to go. All three of us walked out of that school on a high.

Max had made reservations for us at Giardino's, a few minutes' drive from the school in town. We pulled up and got out together.

Inside, I was on watch for Mindy's temper. I knew she'd been under more than the usual amount of attention tonight, and I didn't want her to get tired. But to my surprise, she seemed overjoyed to be there with us. We were seated at a table for three by the window, and I watched the waves crashing against the jetty outside while we waited for our food. The restaurant's other patrons included a few parents, who'd also come from the PTA, and a few people from the town. Some of them I recognized, others, I didn't.

A few strange glances passed in my direction, but I put it out of my mind, assuming they were trying to work out who this stranger was joining the Fircresses for dinner. Max and I shared a salad, as was our habit now, but he enticed me into eating a plate of spaghetti carbonara that was so delicious I couldn't help but make a noise when I tried it.

"Mmmm," I said. "That's just terrific. How's yours, Min?"

"Mmmm," Mindy replied. We laughed together, and I squeezed her hand.

"I guess Mindy and I need to thank you properly, Sophie," said Max. "I never realized just how much you'd be able to help the two of us."

I smiled and looked at my food.

"I really mean it," said Max. "You're a light for both of us. So, forgive us if we don't always get the chance to make it up to you."

I looked up and caught his glance, shining in the candlelight of the restaurant. We both knew what that meant, and I was grateful that he said it. Max really did care for me. He didn't think any of it had been a mistake. He was being as gentle with me as I was with him, making me practically dizzy. We finished our food, and after I'd cleaned up Mindy a little, I excused myself to go to the bathroom.

I went into a stall, and as I did, I heard three or four ladies from another table come in. I recognized their voices from the PTA meeting. They were chattering a little, mostly complaining about a waiter, but settled down a bit, presumably to adjust their makeup in the mirror.

"You suppose that nanny's paying her own bill tonight?" said one of the voices outside, and there was some tittering.

"Hey, if the sheriff's to be believed, Mister Fircress will be paying for four in a couple of months."

"You're kidding. Her and Max?"

"Uh huh. Derrick said it himself. He said that Mister Fircress and Missus Gardner were getting along *so well* he wouldn't be surprised if there were wedding bells in the near future."

Derrick? So one of the moms knew Derrick, and now he was spreading rumors about Max and me. I couldn't believe it. Part of me wanted to storm out and confront them, but I stayed put.

"Shut *up*," said another of the moms, and giggled as she made for the door. "Poor woman probably doesn't even realize Max had Missus Fircress bumped off for her family fortune," she said, leaving. The others laughed cruelly.

"You know..." said one of the others, "...I heard a rumor that Derrick dated that nanny years ago on the mainland."

"You're kidding," said one of the others.

"Scout's honor, hon," the first one replied. "Heard she was a piece of work too. Alice Gardner's kid, remember? Apparently, she won't even talk to her parents now."

"You know that one. She's always been wild. Guess she'd be better suited to raise a feral kid too."

I waited for them to leave. I was shaking with anger, but I let myself calm down before leaving the bathroom. I wasn't about to let some town gossip spoil Mindy's big day. I adjusted my eyeliner, which had been stained by the welling tears in my eyes, and left.

"Oh, good, you're back," said Max, standing up and pulling back my chair for me as I returned. He was such an old-fashioned gentleman like that. "I didn't want you to miss this."

I could already see it coming as I sat down. One of the waiters was bringing a plate to the table. On it was an enormous, round chocolate cake with a candle on the top. I watched it burning brightly in the dingy restaurant as he set it down before Mindy.

"Oh, Max," I said, my heart full to bursting. "You're the

sweetest. Isn't it pretty, Mindy?"

Mindy nodded. She was entranced by the flame in front of her.

"It's a present from me to you," Max said, looking at his daughter. "I know you're working hard to do the best you can at school. And me and...me and Sophie are very proud of you. We love you, Mindy."

Mindy looked at the cake, then at each of us. She smiled slowly, realizing it was for her.

"Well, Min, are you gonna blow it out?" said Max. "Come on. I want to eat that thing!"

Mindy giggled but carried on looking at the cake. I wasn't surprised. I'm sure the flame was igniting her imagination.

"Come on, Min, or it'll go out," I gently encouraged her.

Mindy took a little breath and blew out the candle.

"Good girl!" I said and rubbed her shoulder.

Mindy turned to look at me slowly as if I were a stranger. Her eyes seemed to search my face, old beyond their years.

"Mommy," she said, and I gasped.

Chapter 12

Max

We drove back from the restaurant in silence that night. I couldn't bear to look at her.

The worst thing was that Sophie kept trying to apologize.

"Max," she said. "She wasn't saying it to me. You *know* she wasn't saying it to me."

"Max," she went on. "She was in a familiar place where her mother had taken her before. I bet Winnie even got her a cake there one time."

There was silence between us in the car, and then she said something else that was just too awful to think about.

"You know I'd *never* try to replace..."

"I know." I snapped, just to stop her from talking. Mindy sat next to her in the back of the car. She was still holding the candle from the cake in her hand.

I couldn't say anything to Sophie. I just sat there in silence, confused and hurt—I was hurting everywhere, not just where the scar lay. I looked at it in the mirror a few hours later, staring at myself in the mirror.

The cruel voice came back to me now.

This is what you get, it said. *This is what happens when you ask a woman to take care of your child, when you kiss her...when you want her. How do you feel now? Now your daughter's calling her* **mommy**? *Don't you feel ashamed?*

I tried to put it aside. Had I confused Mindy? Did Mindy somehow know what Sophie and I had done out in the woods? Surely not. And yet, kids had a way of knowing things sometimes, didn't they?

Mindy knew her mother was gone before anyone told her. When they'd brought her to me in the hospital, I'd seen her with a scarf the nurse had given her. Winnie's scarf. The one she'd worn the night of the accident. I still had that thing hung over the rail in my closet.

"I know you want to see mommy," I said. *"I'm sure mommy's okay."*

Mindy looked at me and said one thing. *"Mommy's gone,"* she said.

And that was how I found out my wife was dead.

That was the last time Mindy had spoken.

***

Over the next few days, Sophie and I kept out of sight when Mindy was at school. It had been easy enough to do while she had Mindy to look after. But I didn't want to be alone with her. I didn't know what all of this meant. Worst of all, I felt it was my fault. In the car, I knew what Sophie was trying to say. She'd been trying to tell me she didn't want to replace Winnie in my life, in our lives. She knew she couldn't and would never be a replacement for her. And I knew that Sophie didn't want to. No woman with her courage or strength of character would want that.

But did I? I didn't know, and the confusion and the rage bottled up inside me. I didn't know what to think. Winston had told me he'd be back on Friday evening. Until then, I tried to focus on the business for a while.

***

It was Thursday, the first of Mindy's two school days. She hadn't said anything else since that night in the restaurant. And Sophie and I hadn't been able to look at each other. Now, she was sitting in the kitchen, reading a book. Pretty soon, she'd leave to pick Mindy up. I wasn't even sure I wanted her to go.

My cell phone pinged. I had a text. It was from a number I didn't recognize.

I know something, it said.

I looked at the phone, dumbfounded. I had no idea what that meant. But then the phone pinged again, vibrating in my hand. And another text appeared on the screen.

I know something about the night your wife died, it said.

I didn't know what to think, just stared at the phone while my blood ran cold.

Who is this? I replied.

Breaker's point. One hour, they replied.

I thought about calling Trevor. He would know what to do, considering our conversation a few weeks ago.

"Did anyone ever talk to you about the accident? Anyone from the sheriff's office, I mean," Trevor said, sitting in the car, looking

straight ahead.

"No. I mean, yes. I mean...not really," I replied. "Why?"

There was a long silence between us.

"What I'm about to tell you could really get me into trouble," Trevor said slowly as we looked out at Fairview from his car in the driveway. "Not least of all with you. And if you decide I'm going over the line here, you feel free to tell me."

There was a pall of fear descending on me. I felt sick just thinking about what he might be about to say. "Go on," I said. "I'm listening.

Trevor carried on looking straight ahead. "They say you lost control. They say you were speeding to get to the airfield. But that's not consistent with the crash pattern."

"I've had this conversation before. I know that for sure," I said. I was irritated that Trevor was bringing it up. "Crash patterns don't exactly—"

"I know. They don't always line up with our expectations. You can never really accurately dictate what a vehicle will do at that speed. But it's more than that. The accident report on...on that night, about your wife, it's...inconclusive. Unfinished, some would say. I want to look into it."

"You can do what you want, Trevor. You don't need my permission."

"I know," said Trevor. "Truth is, though, I like you, Max. It would mean a lot."

"I'd prefer we just forgot about it," I said. "I...I want to move on."

"I know you do," replied Trevor. "But, things don't add up."

I sighed, running a hand through my hair. Could I really move on now that I knew there was a possibility that I had been wrong about the accident?

What if all this did was bring up more pain for me? For Mindy?

I wasn't sure what to say, but something in me pulled me towards finding out the truth.

"Well, I happen to like you too, Trevor. If it's my approval you need, you've got it. I guess you can start by looking through the evidence the police collected. I imagine they took a lot of it."

"Yeah, they did," said Trevor. *"So, where is it?"*

I looked down at the text again. At best, it was a scammer, a blackmailer who thought they knew something but didn't. At worst, someone was going to try to hurt me. But I was so confused about Sophie that I couldn't help myself. I drove out to Breaker's Point.

The furthest point west on the island, accessible by road, Breaker's Point, was a dangerous place. A narrow dirt track led down from the pine forests and the airstrip to a clifftop. From there, you could follow a trail down to a narrow beach on the southern side of the island. But Breaker's Point lay beyond, down an old mining trail that cut around Mount Criker, making its way through the forest and over hills to another cliff. And there, you could see the point from the end of the road.

It was a tall, dark spire of jagged rock, rising intimidatingly over the cliffs. Hundreds of rumors abounded among the neighborhood kids about ghosts or lonely lovers who'd frequented its peak in their moment of desperation. You could hardly have chosen a more atmospheric place for a conversation, which made me think it was undoubtedly a bad idea to go. And yet, as I got out of the Jeep and stood, with the motor running, looking out at the enormous basalt tower before me, I couldn't help but feel exhilarated. It felt freeing to be out from under that roof, away from everything. Right there and then, I realized I missed Sophie.

"Admiring the scenery?" a voice said from a hundred yards away or so. I turned back and looked over the hood of the Jeep.

It was Alice Gardner.

She was dressed in dark greens and grays, almost invisible among the trees which stretched up behind her into the mountain. She was wearing a pair of firm hiking boots and had her hands stuffed into an old windbreaker. The wind blew strands of hair around her face and over the top of her beanie.

"Alice?" I said in disbelief.

"The very same," she said, walking towards me. That was Alice: dry as a bone. I'd heard some of the locals refer to her as a one-man Lewis and Clark. It was a stupid name, but kind of true. Alice knew every inch of the island. I wasn't surprised she'd asked to meet me up here. She was fond of tracing the old mining tracks and roads that had once run around the west side of the island.

"I presume this was you?" I said, holding up my phone.

"Sorry for being cryptic," she said, stopping a few feet from my Jeep. "I was distracted."

That seemed to raise a hint of anger in me. "Distracted from telling me about my wife? I've heard all the unpleasant rumors, Alice. Nothing you say can surprise me."

"I was *distracted*..." she said, "...because I've just seen something I don't like up there. You been up there lately, Max?" She pointed back at the east side of the island.

"Not lately," no, I said.

"Signs up there now. *No trespassing*. I've lived on this island for fifty years, and no one's ever laid claim to that side of the island. It's a nature reserve, not a goddam development site."

"Why don't you cut to the chase..." I said, "...and tell me *exactly* what it is you think you know about Winnie."

"How's my daughter getting along?" she said, looking away from me to the waves crashing on Breaker's Point. "Got a right to know, don't I?"

"You're welcome to visit any time, Alice. All of you are. You know that. It's not Sophie's fault her family doesn't want her around."

I thought I saw a hint of something painful cross her face when I said that, and then it returned to how it was before: hard, expressionless, aged a little by years of hard living and working in the wilderness. "I just want to make sure she's been keeping good company," she said. "God knows that moron made her life difficult enough. I don't need another man making things hard on her."

"I don't want anything for Sophie, but what's good for her," I said.

She sneered a little. "I bet. Anyways, I was thinking about you two after I saw you palling around in the diner the other night—"

"You mean, that night you interrupted her and made her upset?" I interrupted.

She paused at that, then carried on. "I was thinking about you two because Trevor's had a lot to say about you at home recently. About your wife. About the night she passed."

So Trevor had been talking to Alice about Winnie's death. I sighed. "What do you have to say, Alice? Getting kind of dark out here, isn't it? Mindy will be getting home soon."

"Got a nanny, ain't she?" said Alice, a little rougher this time. "The point is, I told Trevor this, and now I'm telling you. He's right."

There was silence between us. "Anything else?" I said. "You brought me up here to tell me you think he's right?"

Alice shook her head. "Look, ain't no secret that Sophie and I had words back in the day. I've got regrets about my family, Max. Sure you have as well. But I always looked out for her. And when that piece of...when our sheriff moved back here, I was plenty mad about it."

I didn't say anything, just looked at her. Alice was never one to wear her heart on her sleeve, but she seemed practically emotional at this point.

"So the night your wife died, god rest her soul, I happened to go down to the station. Officer Park was in, and I wanted to speak to Derrick. I wanted to tell him to piss off while he still had a chance to. I didn't want him here, dragging up the past. Anyway, I got there, and you'll never guess what."

"What, Alice?" I said. "What?"

"Wasn't there. Officer Park said he was out near the airstrip on patrol. Near the road where the car fell off. Funny that, ain't it? Like he knew it was going to happen."

My heart thudded in my chest, a dull thump like a muffled drum. "What are you saying?"

"I'm saying that a few things don't add up, as Trevor puts it to me. The first one being that Derrick's got no paperwork about any of it. You know that already, though."

"Yeah," I said. "He's looking into it."

"And we know Derrick was out there at the time of the accident, and he's on record as the first on the scene."

"What else do we know, Alice? What else do you know?"

She sighed and paused. "Not a lot, to be honest. But I've got some ideas."

"I'd love to hear them. I'd love to hear them quickly, too; I'm pretty busy at the moment."

Alice sighed and stepped away. She was leaving. "I know your family wasn't altogether on the same page, Max. I know Winnie and Winston were at odds. After all, Winnie wanted the east side of this island undeveloped, didn't she?"

"What are you insinuating? Just who the hell do you think you—"

"And I know that your wife would want her wishes honored in that regard. She wouldn't want her brother doing anything out there...building out there. Cutting down the trees. Harming the wildlife."

"That doesn't have anything to do with her death. And besides, he would never do that," I replied. I was all but finished talking to her and popped the door on my Jeep.

"Then why's Winston Locklow's name on those signs?" she said, wandering off into the darkness.

Chapter 13

Sophie

The more I thought about it, the more I couldn't believe it. But I began to realize that I'd crossed a line with Mindy.

It started with me noticing little things. Like how she hugged me in the morning as we woke up. Then, I started to notice more. She showed me everything she did and wanted my approval. And then there were the drawings. She showed pictures of me, her, and Max together, like a family. Sure, we were always going to be close. But how close should we be? I'd never discussed it with Max. I never thought we'd need to. When I met Mindy, she'd been so distant that I don't think Max realized it could happen.

One of the first things I learned when I read for my degree was about attachment. When kids feel secure with their caregivers, they don't just need to stay with them. They explore, knowing that because there's a nest, a place they feel comfortable and safe, they can stray from it and discover new things. Mindy was exploring now, drawing, playing, and talking because she was with someone who made her feel safe and secure.

But Mindy was really starting to look at me like I was her mom.

And I just couldn't have that. She might have started to talk, but that made it even more important that she didn't misunderstand or misjudge our relationship. If I let her do that, I'd undo every bit of good work we'd done.

What would happen if I stopped working for her dad?

So when I went to get Mindy from school on Friday, I made sure to be clear about my boundaries.

"How was your day, Mindy?" I asked.

She smiled and jogged a little toward me, holding her bag and sketchbook in one hand. She dropped them and stretched out her arms when she got to where I was standing by the school gates. I could tell she wanted a hug from me, but quick as I could, I rebuffed her, picking up her things and beginning to walk to the car.

Mindy kept reaching for my hand in the car whenever it moved to the glove box. I knew that physical contact had become a part of our relationship, and I wanted to limit it. We were driving out across the hills now. Fairview was almost there.

"Mindy, don't do that, please," I said, and she huffed and folded her arms.

Mindy moaned and shifted in her seat. She felt strange.

"Mindy, I need to ask you what you said during dinner the other day. Do you remember what you said?"

Mindy looked at me but didn't say anything. The suspicion in her eyes made me wince a little.

"I want to help you understand why you said what you said. It's okay that you said it. But it isn't true, is it? You don't think I'm your mommy, do you?"

Mindy didn't say anything, just looked at her hands,

interlacing the fingers.

"Because I'm not, okay? I'm Sophie. I'm your nanny. Do you understand that?"

She wouldn't even look at me. Back to square one. We were pulling up the driveway now, and I was relieved to see Mrs. Langley's car outside.

"Mrs. Langley?" I asked as I walked into the house. "You there?"

"Yes, dear," she said. A short, plump woman with graying hair emerged from the kitchen in a black smock and a pair of moon boots. "Just waiting for the laundry to be done, really. You sure have cleaned up the place a bit since it was just the other two! And how are you, Missy?"

Mindy smiled and waved.

"Quite a change in this one lately, isn't there?" Mrs. Langley said.

I smiled guiltily, then hid my smile altogether. I had to learn to stop taking praise for Mindy's behavior in front of her. It only reinforced the idea that I wanted her to be close to me. And as much as that was true, it wasn't right.

"Mind if I leave her with you?" I asked. "I need a little air. We've had a funny old week around here. Think I might go down to the beach for an hour or so."

Mrs. Langley happily agreed. She always wanted to spend time with Mindy, even if the feeling wasn't exactly mutual. Mindy spun around to look at me in protest, but I turned around and got out of the house fast. It felt so unnatural to leave her like that, but a bit of space was in order. It would help Mindy know I was only there to care for her. That would be good for us. I knew it would. And good for Max, too.

I was tired of walking in the hills and wanted to go down to the beach. There were four beaches on Criker's Isle. One to the east, one out near Breaker's Point, and two out by town, the closest of which was twenty minutes walk or so from Fairview. I looked at the fields beside me as I made my way down the paths. The gorse bushes and brackens were already starting to brown, and a cold wind ran through me. Max had got me a windbreaker from town the other day. I knew he cared for me, and still wanted to look after me. And yet...

What was the point of anything without him, without the intimacy we'd already shared? It had been nearly two weeks since we went climbing together. I couldn't remember feeling so special to anyone in my life. And I'd ruined it. How? By being there for his daughter when she needed someone? Part of me wanted to resent Max for the way he was treating me, but I buried it. Resentment wanted to settle in me and think cruel thoughts, but I suppressed them. Deep down, I just couldn't bear to think of life without his touch again.

I was at the bottom of the hill and crossed the main road, hopping on the grassy verge, which dropped onto the beach. There, I wandered up and down for a little while, looked at the dark cliffs rising above me and then at sea. The sand was a tinge of gray in the failing light, and I watched the setting sun drawing white streaks across the dark, muddy waters of the sea. I used to feel I could see my fate when I looked there, knowing that the mainland lay just a few miles away, a promise of freedom and escape. But you can never escape anything. I should have known that before I isolated myself.

Suddenly I was startled when I heard the blip of a siren behind me. I turned around, fear running through me, freezing me to the spot. Then I relaxed. It was Trevor—the big dolt. He was waving at me, his broad, triangular frame easily visible by the roadside.

"Sophie! What are you doing down here? I went up to the

house. The old lady told me you were down here."

"You're gonna have to get a different car when you want to come see me from now on, Trevor," I said. "I keep thinking you're someone else."

"If I had a dollar every time someone told me that..." He nodded, a concerned look on his face. "Well, guess who I came to talk to you about, as a matter of fact. You know he's been talking about you in town?"

I remembered the parents in the bathroom at Giardino's and nodded. "Yeah. I know. Let him talk. I don't care."

"Well, I need you to care," replied Trevor. "Because some things have been...confusing me. You remember I was going to look into...into Winnie?"

"Yeah. Did you find something?"

He gave me a searching look. "Sure did. Or, rather, didn't. The file's missing from the accident. And now mom's saying—"

"Mom? You talked to mom about this?"

"She talked to me. She told me some stuff, sis. You know she went to tell Derrick where to go on the night of the accident?"

"No way. Why would she do that?"

"Why d'you think? She loves you, Sophie. She wasn't gonna let the guy just walk around town without giving him a piece of her mind. You know mom's got an unpaid parking ticket from Derrick for parking by a hiking trail a few winters back? She keeps telling him to arrest her over it."

I couldn't deny it; I was ever so slightly impressed with my mom.

"Only problem is, when she went to tell him what-for, he wasn't there. He'd already gone."

I remembered something. "Wait. Trevor. He was first on the scene, wasn't he?"

"Yep. As far as I know. Sheriff Park said he did such a good job with it that he could write up the file and everything. Not like I'm going to ask him about it now that the file's gone. But, see where I'm going with all of this?"

"Any other reason he was out at the airstrip?"

"No idea since there's no file. He told me he was having a cup of coffee in the diner. There's a problem with that."

"Let me guess," I said, looking out where Bushey's would be in the distance. "It was closed that night."

"Yeah..." said Trevor. "How'd you guess that one?"

Eleven years ago, when we'd lived together on the mainland, Derrick had once told me he was working late at a gas station. I'd gone down there to surprise him and discovered it was closed. He'd been at the bar instead. The guy just wasn't a good liar.

"Lucky, I guess. So, what are you going to do?"

"What I came here to do. Ask for your help."

"Me?" I was confused. "Why would I be able to help, Trevor? You're the law. You work at his office, and you're a deputy."

"He doesn't trust me, sis. But he trusts you, or at least, he believes you trust him. Creep's always telling me how you'll see sense and get back with him one day."

"Yeah, well, if you think I'm going anywhere near that psychopath again, you've got another thing coming. There's no way."

"If you would just talk to him—"

"No, Trevor."

He saw that I meant it and held up his hands. Then his eyes narrowed.

"You know, back then, when you left? When I gave you the money?"

I looked at him. "What?"

"He...he hurt you, didn't he?"

I looked at Trevor and folded my arms. Then I looked away. "It wasn't anything serious. But I guess it could have been. Yeah. He hurt me. It's what he does. And he'll do it again if I get close to him. So no, Trevor, I'm not talking to Derrick."

Trevor nodded. "Alright, then. I guess I'm on my own."

"You're not on your own, Trevor. But you're not—"

He'd ignored me. In fact, he was already walking away. As he did, I heard him muttering to himself.

"I'll get you, you son of a bitch," he said.

Chapter 14

Max

That Friday, I came back and found Mindy and Mrs. Langley by themselves. I'd been out to see the signs on the eastern side of the island for myself. It had taken me three hours to get up and down again, but Alice was right. Winston had bought land on the eastern front for reasons unknown to me. In fact, he'd purchased most of the land outside the nature reserve. I was amazed he hadn't told me. It had been Winnie's favorite place in the whole world.

I knew Winston would be back today, so I didn't say anything. I was sure he could explain it all to me. And besides, it was his money. I'm sure he was planning to do something good with it.

Luckily, I'd get to ask him. I got back to the house at around seven.

"Mrs. Langley? How are you doing? Where's Sophie?"

Mrs. Langley huffed, lifting Mindy off her knee and setting her down. Mindy scrambled off like a cat that didn't want to be pet.

"Well, it's just the strangest thing. Miss Gardner said she was going down to the beach. Then her brother called and said he wanted to talk to her. I've just no idea where she could have gone. I trust everything's alright?"

"Sure it is. Sophie can have a night off if she wants." I almost felt grateful we didn't have to meet eyes guiltily again over dinner.

"There's something else, Mr. Fircress. It's your brother-in-law. He's in the living room."

"Here? Already? Well, I suppose I'd better get in there."

I crossed the kitchen and passed through the dining room, where Winston had slung his travel case. I picked it up and put it by the table before I went in. "How are you, Winston?"

"Maxy boy!" he said, spinning around. I could see he'd been looking at the papers on my desk. There were no lights but a lamp in the corner, casting a dim, golden glow over Winston's shiny suit.

"Good flight?"

"As ever, old man. Little bumpy, though. Don't you ever think about building these simple country folk a proper airport?"

I laughed. "I'm not sure we really need one, Winston. I hardly think a Boeing 747 landing on the south coast would greatly improve the scenery."

"I suppose not, I suppose not," chuckled Winston, reclining back onto one of the couches. He narrowly missed Mindy's sketchbook, which he absentmindedly picked up and dropped onto the table, far away from him. On its front page was a rabbit nibbling at the grass.

"I see that nanny of yours has finally managed to teach her how to draw," said Winston. "Pretty young thing, isn't she?"

"Well, sure. We're all big fans of Sophie around here," I said.

"She's good for Mindy as well."

"Oh yeah? Nurturing, hm? I get it. Must be nice for you, Max, having a...feminine presence around the house. Of course, no one could ever replace Winnie." At this, he looked a little sad, and his eyes widened. "My twin was irreplaceable."

"She was," I said. "Say, Winston."

"Hm?" he said, stirred out of his reverie.

"There are a couple of things I wanted to ask you about. See here," I said, getting up and going to my desk. "I've got quarterly reports back to the last five now...that was about when I started stepping back from it all. I've got some *serious* mishandling of the figures here, Winston."

"Oh? Let me take a look?" he said disinterestedly.

"It's not that I'm not happy about us maintaining the profit margin," I said as I handed him the papers. "It's just, none of it makes *sense* to me. Look at the third quarter of last year. How are we spending less on materials and manufacturing *more* chairs? Someone in accounting needs to get their head straightened out. Either that..." I said, "...or there's something I don't know about. Either way, I hoped you'd be the one to tell me."

"You're quite right, Max," said Winston, pulling out a pair of glasses from his pocket and perching them on the end of his nose. "This doesn't make any sense. Look, I promise you, I'll look into it. But right now, I'm a little busy. How about I come down sometime over the weekend, and we look at it together?"

"That's not going to do, Winston. What's going on with the figures?"

He stopped and flapped his arms out beside him, dropping the papers I'd assembled in an untidy pile on the couch. "Max," he said. "*Max*," he repeated, beaming that happy smile. "Aren't you happy with the way things are going? The shareholders' meeting last Summer was just—"

"I'm more than happy, Winston. But you know how I am. Your sister and I founded this company together. And I need to make sure it's being run properly. No cutting corners. No turning a profit while decimating some forest."

"Well, you know very well, Max, I would never be so thoughtless as to go against Winnie's principles...against *your* principles. I love the environment just as much as you do."

"Is that why you've bought the eastern slopes?" I said quietly.

There was silence in the living room. Winston was frozen in his spot, still smiling at me. Smiling away.

He nodded once, decisively. He was still smiling, but there was something else in his shiny, dark eyes. So much like Winnie's eyes, but more...intense.

"That's exactly why, Max. Exactly why. You know that my poor twin loved that part of the world, don't you? It was her favorite part. And believe me, I intend to keep it safe. I plan to put it in an easement so no one can touch it. Oh, there are all kinds of people in the world, Max, and when they see a bit of land like that, they get it into their heads to do all kinds of things."

I nodded. "Even build on it," I said. "Build roads, houses. A resort, maybe. Whatever that might do to the environment."

"Exactly. So I took it upon myself to acquire that land."

"How did you manage to do that, Winston?"

Winston stayed there, smiling his big smile, his eyes shining brighter in the lamplit room.

"Life's all about connections, isn't it? After all, you know that more than anyone. After all..." he continued, easing himself onto his feet, "...without Winnie's money, you'd never have started this business. Never forget that, Max."

"Never do, Winston," I said quietly. His words were a weapon, a warning. They said, *don't ask me any more about this; just don't.* I relented for the time being.

"Now," said Winston, stretching and yawning, almost catlike. "I'm rather tired. Think I'll go up to the guesthouse."

"I'll have Mrs. Langley bring some food and things up for you."

"Just fabulous. I really do appreciate it so much, Max. Winnie would be so happy if she could see you accommodating me right now. She really would."

He went out of the room to collect his bag, but I stayed in the living room, fists balled and boiling.

I looked at the clock. It was almost half past seven. Where was Sophie?

Chapter 15

Sophie

Every town has a place like this. Every town. I swear it.

This one was Fairtown's. It had been here since I was a child. I don't know how many times I'd been told not to go in. It was called The Red Rod.

The Red Rod was a bar, although you could hardly tell. From the outside, it looked fairly charming, with a curved, paned window like the side of a beer glass and a faint glow from within. Pity that when you did go in, you realized the faint glow occurred because the glass was so dirty.

I'd been here before, of course. First with a few friends, then once or twice with Derrick. He'd always been able to scam the bartender into getting me drinks. At the time, I thought it was normal. I thought all sixteen-year-olds bought their fifteen-year-old girlfriends' whiskey sours. I guess I was wrong. I thought about the fact that Mindy was just six years younger than I was the last time I was in here and how I was fifteen years older. And then I took another gulp of the whiskey.

I was sick of it all, sick of everything. Sick of being afraid of

Derrick, reminded of him just by the sound of Trevor's car, by Trevor's crazy story. And I was sick of Max, sick of him blaming me for something I had no control over, sick of the guilt I felt for showing some love to his little girl. I just wanted him to know I cared. So yeah, I was at The Red Rod.

I looked around. Two guys sat in the corner, local fishermen, I guessed. They wore the gear, anyway, and were deep in their cups. At the window, a young couple mooned over one another. On their way home from a movie, I imagined.

I hadn't come here to get drunk—I don't think I'd been to a bar in years. I'd come here because I thought no one would find me. Still, after the day I'd had, avoiding Max, Mindy, and the beach with Trevor, I'd earned a beer, for sure. The clock said eight, and I felt sorry for Mrs. Langley. She'd be expecting me back by now.

The bottle sat in front of me, its cheery red logo making me feel even more sorry for myself. As I took a deep draught, a Steve Earle song started to play on the radio.

I let myself sigh, a deep sigh, and my shoulders sagged. I felt exhausted by it all. So exhausted that I didn't even notice when the barman looked up in front of me and nodded.

"Evening, sheriff. What'll you have?"

"I'm off for the night, Marv. Guess I'll have what the lady's having."

I looked up. Derrick stood by the bar. He'd changed out of his sheriff's uniform. He winked at me.

"What do you want, Derrick?"

He said nothing, just smirked.

"Nice to see you too, Soph. Exploring your old haunts?"

I was afraid, so afraid. I looked at the couple by the window. They didn't notice. How could they? They couldn't see what I saw. Couldn't see the look in his eye as he sat next to me. The barman set a beer down in front of him, then made for the back room.

"I only ever came here with you, as I recall."

"Had a great time though, didn't you? Look, Soph, I wanted to apologize for sneaking up on you the other day. Let me get you a beer. Let's talk."

"I don't want to talk. I want you to leave me alone. How did you know I'd be here?"

"I didn't, of course. I come here most Fridays now. A lonely life on this island, isn't it?"

He sat on the stool, but he was turned towards me. My brain was screaming at me to run, but somehow I felt frozen to the spot. And my mind felt like it was somewhere else, a hundred miles away from here and ten years in the past, shouting, telling him to get away from me. I couldn't stand the sight of him.

"Still, Sophie, I don't always come here. Maybe something in my heart was telling me to come tonight. Maybe some part of me did know you'd be here. Maybe I just wanted to see you."

"Oh yeah? I thought you'd have given up on me by now, seeing as you've been telling the whole town me and Max are an item now."

"Well, if the shoe fits, huh?" He laughed—a harsh, metallic laugh—and scratched his stubble.

"Yeah. Sure. Still, no one ever fit anything on you, Derrick. You always had a way of slipping out where the law was concerned. No wonder you're so good at it."

"Wow, sure got a mouth on you. Mister Fircress left you alone tonight, huh? Not very wise of him, was it?"

Despite his jovial tone, there was cruelty in his eyes. I turned and kept my gaze straight ahead, trying to focus on a half-empty bottle on the bar shelf. If I let him lock eyes with me again, I'd only feel more afraid of him.

"Do us all a favor, Derrick," I said, gritting my teeth. "Leave me the hell alone. I've got no business talking to you, and neither do you with me."

"Woah, looks like you've had a little too much to drink tonight, Soph. Better watch your mouth."

"I've had *half a beer*, you moron."

"I've seen a lot of girls go this way, Sophie," he said. "They have a drink, and all of a sudden, there's a commotion. Someone gets hurt, or someone lashes out. Can be a pretty tricky situation. Especially if, I don't know, you work with kids or something."

I was looking at the exit now, past him, past his little, piggish eyes. The couple by the window was staring at us. They could tell we were in a confrontation. That was good. He wouldn't try anything here. Would he?

"If you don't mind, Derrick, I'm going home now."

"You sure?" said Derrick, a fake look of concern crossing his round, tanned face. "Not going to put that little girl to bed with a bellyful of beer in you, are you?"

I stopped halfway off the stool. I slid down, standing in front of him, resisting the temptation to slap that stupid face of his.

I made to walk past him and get out of there, but he caught me gently enough, with his hand on my arm.

"Take my advice, girl. If we just—"

"Let her go, Derrick."

It was Max.

He stood in the doorway in nothing but a pair of jeans and his plaid shirt.

"Well, *Max*! This isn't what it seems like. Fortunately, she's only had one drink. Hope you don't take it personally or nothing. Seems like old Sophie here's had a rough day. We were just talking about it, in fact."

I looked at Max and held his gaze.

Help me. Please.

He was already coming towards us.

"Sophie's allowed to have a night off, Derrick. Mindy's with my housekeeper now."

"If it's fine with you, Max, it's fine with me. I'm just saying. I personally wouldn't be happy if my nanny were at the bar while my kid was at home with the rest of the help."

"Sheriff, if you had a child to look after, I think we can all agree that would be trouble enough." I saw Derrick practically spit out his beer at that.

"Max," I said, trying to stop him.

"Ain't no need to be rude," said Derrick, wounded now, feigning injury. "I was just—"

"Whatever you were doing, it doesn't matter. Sophie's coming home with me now."

"Well, is she?" snapped Derrick, with a mean look on his face. He and Max were less than two feet away from one another, and it frightened me. Max looked like he was going to knock Derrick out there and then. He put his hand on me, his touch bringing warmth to my shocked system. We started to walk out before Derrick opened his fat mouth once again.

"Be careful on the roads, Max. Wouldn't want anything bad to happen, would we?"

Max stopped dead in his tracks. I could see his fists had balled, and his face had reddened. Then he said nothing, and we walked out of the bar together.

***

Max remained quiet the whole way home in the Jeep. I kept looking at him. Was he angry at me? Did he blame me for what had just happened?

As we pulled in and got out, Fairview sat silently before us. Max unlocked the front door and went in. Mrs. Langley got up from where she was sitting in the kitchen.

"Oh, Mister Fircress, thank goodness you're home. Are you alright, Sophie?"

I was too ashamed to answer, but Max did on my behalf. "She's fine, Barbara. Sophie was just taking a walk. Eh, Sophie?"

I nodded.

"Well, Mindy's safe in bed and just gone off to sleep," said Mrs. Langley. "I'll be heading off now if that's alright. It's almost eight, anyhow."

"That's just fine. Thank you for looking after Mindy."

Mrs. Langley left, closing the door behind her. After a moment of silence, Max went and locked the door.

"Max, I'm so sorry. I just...I didn't know where I was at. It's not...I know I've done something awful tonight, Max. I'll go."

My words seemed to bring him back to me. He turned and looked at me from the hallway. "What do you mean, go?"

"I can't...I can't stay, I mean, after this. After you had to come get me like that..."

He put his hands on my shoulders and held me close and tight, and I rested my head on his shoulders. I felt the tears come and felt them wetting his shirt collar. "Don't you ever go anywhere," he said. "Don't you *dare* go."

"Max?" I said, looking up at him, watching his kind, concerned eyes as they studied me.

"Sophie. I don't..."

He cleared his throat, emotional.

"I don't care that you went out. I don't care. God knows I haven't...haven't done right by you, leaving you alone with Min this week. You needed me. I wasn't there. I'm sorry for not talking to you. I'm sorry you found yourself alone with that...that man."

I shook my head. "Don't apologize, Max. You're wonderful. You've both been so good to me. How can I ever say thank you?"

"You can sit with me a little while in the living room."

I glowed from the inside when he said that.

We went and sat down on the couch. He sat next to me, holding hands. "I like you so much, Sophie. More than...more than I could ever say," he said.

"Max, I like you too. Really like you. You make it all okay. You make it feel right to be here, on Criker's Isle, I mean. But what Mindy said..."

"Mindy can tell us what she meant when she's ready," he said. "But it doesn't change the way I feel about you. It just changes the way I feel about myself, I guess."

"How's that?"

"It makes me feel bad. It makes me guilty."

"Of what, Max? Guilty of what?"

And then, he kissed me again.

I reeled from the impression his lips left on mine, and when he paused, I took his face in my hands. I felt the rough stubble on his cheeks and turned his head to face me properly as I kneeled on the sofa, a little above him, showering him with my adoration.

"Sophie, I—"

"Don't," I said. "Take what you want. What you've wanted since we first met."

He didn't disappoint me.

He reached his arms around me, practically lifting me into his lap while our lips locked together in a magical union. I wrapped my legs around him, and my hands traced his strong jaw, neck, throat, and shoulders. *All mine...*

While I pressed his back against the couch with the force of my passion, Max's hands reached for my waist. He held me gracefully and gently, making me feel the full power of my own body, ready to please him, to be pleased by him. I could feel his cock was hard already in his pants, and I happily pressed my hips against his, so he could feel my full womanhood, already getting wet and warm for him. Max's hands finally found my breasts, massaging them, and I moaned and growled in my throat, hungry for him, desperate. He smiled between kisses, sensing my pleasure and responding in kind. I felt his raging hard-on press up against me.

While recklessly dry-humping him, I began to undo the shirt he was wearing, my mouth breaking free of his and traveling down to his chest. I could hardly bear the delight when he finally threw me over onto my back, watching his muscled torso as he adjusted himself over me, like a panther waiting to devour his prey.

Now, his kisses were a little rough, and wild, and his mouth was searching down, lifting my top and kissing my stomach. My mind spanned around in circles as he deftly unbuttoned my jeans and removed them, revealing my panties. I knew what he was about to do and threaded one of my hands through his fair hair, adjusting a cushion for one of them.

My panties slid off, and Max buried his face between my legs, his tongue making a gentle, upward motion to see if I was wet enough. He could have taken me there and then if he wanted, but he stopped.

"Ever since I saw you wearing that dress to the PTA..." he said, "...I've wondered what it would be like to do this."

He began tracing the gentlest little circles around my clit, awakening a part of me I hadn't felt in years. As if by instinct, my thighs lifted themselves to close gently around his head, my hand in his hair a mindful guide.

"Oh, Max..." I said, breathless and dizzy, "...that's so good."

But it wasn't going to be enough, I knew.

"Fuck me," I said. "Fuck me right now," I said again.

When I saw him rear up to unzip his jeans, the sight of his cock was heavenly. He was even harder for me than he'd been in the forest after our climb.

Max leaned over me, resting himself gently against my hips. With one hand, he held my head and pressed it into his chest until I felt so safe I knew I could take everything he was about to give me. With his other hand, he teased the lips of my pussy until I was dripping and quietly moaning. I was ready to receive him.

"Please, please, Max."

He eased himself into me slowly, and a sigh of relief ran through me. God, it felt good to be had by him. Max eased further and further inside with slow, simple thrusts until he filled me with his enormous dick. But it wasn't enough, and I felt him hold my hands and kiss me, press me into the couch, as he began to angle himself forward and stimulate my clit.

"Oh, Jesus, that's so much, so much," I said. I didn't know what I was thinking anymore. I could hardly remember where I was, except that I had to be quiet. Max was silently roaring with pleasure above me, whispering into my ear now and then, "You feel so good."

The angle at which he fucked me was perfect, as though he already knew all my secrets. I knew I would come, and I started to try to tell him.

But Max kept diving into me until I saw stars. I felt my eyes bulge a little and shook my head, and he reached out to put a loving hand on my mouth.

Even so, I still audibly squealed as I finally gave way for him, coming at just the same time he did, until my whole body quivered, not mine anymore but his, and his, mine, and we lay together on the sofa, panting and sweaty and utterly at peace.

Chapter 16

Max

I woke up in the morning with the sun streaming through my bedroom windows. I rubbed my eyes and turned over sleepily. Suddenly, I sat up and felt my chest.

The scar didn't pain me at all.

I turned to my side, looking for Sophie. She wasn't there. I'd seen her set the alarm on her phone for early in the morning last night. We'd wanted to sleep together in my bed but didn't want any chance of Mindy seeing us. I felt sure she'd crept back to her own room.

Outside, the sun blazed. I went to the window and felt the glass. It was a cold day out there, for sure, but still pretty bright. Hopefully, it would warm up. I knew just how I wanted to spend the day with my girls as I was beginning to think of them.

I went across the hallway to Mindy's room first. Peeking through the door, I watched for a few moments. She was sleeping contentedly. In her arms, she held a bear, blue with a white bow around his neck. Mindy had gone through so many bears, and I hadn't seen her play with one or sleep with one in years, but I was pretty sure this particular incarnation's name was Charlie. I left them together and headed stealthily down the stairs.

I had a couple of things to do on the second floor of the house. First, I turned on the eco-burner. Connected to a furnace, it supplemented the solar heaters on top of the house by heating us using wood and other biomass from sustainable sources. It was turned low, and I raised the temperature a little. Then, I gently opened the door to Sophie's room.

I'd never been in it since she moved in with us—it was her private space, and I didn't want to disturb it—but I couldn't resist getting a look at her as she lay on her side, with one hand under her head and the other pulling the comforter around her. Her bare, white shoulder lay above her, illuminated by the sun, and I bent down to kiss it as I stroked her auburn hair a little. I placed one more kiss on her cheek, feeling delighted and warmed by the sight of her before leaving.

Downstairs, I got to work on some breakfast for the two of them. It was a Saturday, which, up until a few years ago, had been pancake day in our house. I decided it was about time to revive that tradition, and I got to work. In no time at all, the thick batter was gently sizzling away in a skillet while I struggled with the coffee machine and took deep draughts from the thermos of tea I'd made for myself.

I put a dish on the hotplate and began stacking the pancakes when a rustling noise distracted me. I went into the dining room and saw Mindy, in her pajamas and pink robe, with Charlie on her lap. She looked through the stack of papers and magazines untidily over the table. I went over to her and bent to kiss her forehead.

"What are you looking for, Min?" I asked. "Want something to read?"

She stared intensely at the stack of magazines as though

making her mind up about something. Then, she took a deep breath.

"I-I want...to go back to school on Mondays a-again," she said. I was stunned. It had been the first complete sentence she'd said in three years. And, aside from the episode at the restaurant, I don't think I'd heard my daughter's voice in such a long time.

It was a struggle for her, but it didn't sound like she had any difficulties with her speech. I decided to press her. "Why's that, Mindy?"

She looked in front of her again, frowning with concentration. I could tell it was costing her an immense effort to break her habit of silence. "Want to...be normal..."

"You are normal, honey." It was Sophie, standing in the doorway in her emerald robe. Her eyes met mine, and we smiled at each other. "In fact..." said Sophie, as she strode to the table and sat down opposite Mindy, "...you're just perfect the way you are. But if you want to go to school, I guess we'll have to see what your daddy says, won't we?" She turned and winked at me mischievously.

I was overjoyed, so overjoyed I was having trouble talking myself. "Well...sure. If it's what you want, Mindy. I bet there's gonna be a lot to catch up on. You sure you're ready for that?"

Mindy smiled and nodded sagely, glancing at Charlie as if for reassurance.

"School it is, I guess. Sure you won't be lonely, Sophie?" I said, looking at her with a mischievous glint in my eye.

We might be getting some more time to ourselves...

Sophie shook her head. "I'll be just fine."

I returned to the kitchen, brought out the pancake dish, and topped the table with some plates, forks, and maple syrup. Sophie helped Mindy serve herself and topped her own modest short stack with yogurt and blueberries.

"So, who wants to go sailing today?" I said. Sophie's eyes widened.

"Sailing?" she said. "You have a boat?"

"Sure," I said. "It's about the only thing I looked forward to when we moved out here. And the water looks calm today, what with the sun out of the clouds and everything. How about it, Min?"

Mindy looked down for a minute, then back up again.

"Can...Charlie come?" she said, proffering the bear, and we both laughed.

***

We drove down to the jetty. Sophie was wearing one of my chunky sweaters, which was adorably oversized on her. Over that, she wore a parka and a pair of gloves. On the other hand, Mindy was in her favorite jumpsuit, complete with the works: hat, scarf, gloves, and an enormous puffy coat. Sophie had insisted on making sure she stayed warm, no matter what. And I'd tied a pair of sturdy boots to her feet, so there was no chance of her slipping.

The *Puffin* was a light, sturdy sloop, easy to manage. I could probably have sailed her by myself, but Sophie insisted on helping. On the private jetty, we worked quickly, hauling up the fenders from the side of the boat and casting off, untying the ropes looped around the poles of the walkway. I fired up the motor, and we were off. Once we were out in open water, I could usually manage the *Puffin* with sailcraft alone, but in the bay, it was more useful to maneuver with the boat's engine.

I watched Mindy and Sophie at the front as we pulled out of

the harbor. Sophie was tightly holding Mindy to her, protective. I glanced at the two of them while keeping an eye on my surroundings. The wind whipped my face, but it exhilarated me. And I was happy to see Sophie pointing out the coastal features of Criker to Mindy. She pointed the landmarks, down from Breaker's Point to the cliffs, then on behind us to Bushey's diner and Fairview, nestled high up on the hills off to my right. Sophie was delighted at how Mindy repeated the landmarks' names after her. She was still pretty quiet but hearing her voice brought a sense of peace to my heart. Eventually, Mindy was happy to stroll up and down the boat by herself, and Sophie walked over to where I stood at the wheel of the ship.

"We've got a lot to be thankful for, don't we?" she said. "Even if it is freezing out here, it's still beautiful." Noticing that Mindy's attention was turned away toward the horizon, she planted a quick kiss on my cheek. I wanted more but decided not to risk it.

"We sure do," I said. "She's talking again. Actually talking to both of us."

"Well, I'm not going to push her on it," said Sophie wisely as she watched Mindy with her brilliant green eyes. "She may decide she doesn't want to talk at school or to her teachers. What's important is she trusts us now."

"And it's thanks to you," I said, looking at her. I meant it. Sophie had given me back my daughter. She'd also given me back a part of myself I thought was lost forever. I felt tenderness for her I'd not felt in years. "The pair of us owe a lot to you."

"I'm sorry I ran out the other night," she said, looking at the gray waves cresting in our wake. "I didn't mean to worry you. And I didn't mean to leave her, either."

"You didn't do any of those things," I said. "Well..." I added, correcting myself, "...you did kinda worry me a little. But I think I deserved it, honestly."

"You sure didn't," replied Sophie. "You think you deserve a hard life, Max. But you don't. And you deserve someone who's on your side. I always want to be that person. So from now on, I promise to talk to you when things are bothering me. Even if that scares me."

I nodded and reached out to squeeze her hand. I turned the boat to the north, so we could coast in the waves for a little while. I could tell Sophie had more to say, so I waited.

"Max, last night...I don't know what it means yet."

"Me neither. I know I want it again, though."

Sophie grinned. Was it the cold that was reddening her cheeks or the thought of us being in bed together again? "Me too," she said quietly.

As I turned the boat around, Criker's Isle loomed up before us in all its stunning beauty. For a while, we just stood there, all three of us, staring at Mount Criker rising from the mists around its lush, green foothills.

"This is a beautiful place," said Sophie, looking at it. "I never realized that when I was growing up here."

"Winnie always wanted to move us here," I explained. "I could never really see why until the first time I came in on the ferry. Then I knew I'd want to be here for the rest of my life."

"Really?" Sophie asked, happy. Then, she looked at Mindy. "What about you, Mindy? Do you want to stay here forever?"

Mindy nodded, then she thought about it for a bit. "Except when I go to a big school. And college. And become an astronaut."

Sophie and I smiled and giggled when she said that. "Okay..." I said, "...but then? Once you're an astronaut?"

Mindy looked at both of us. "As long as I'm with you two," she said a little bashfully.

I couldn't help but kneel and hold her. Mindy wrapped her arms around me. She still had a faraway look in her eye, but when Sophie kneeled too and wrapped one arm around Mindy and one around me, it felt like everything was right. Above us, the sky began to gray a little, and waves had begun to gently rock the ship. But I knew it would still be safe to land. Looking at the two people in my arms, I realized they meant the world to me.

Chapter 17

Sophie

The weekend passed quickly. Max and I spent the night together again, sneaking up to my room this time. We thought there would be less chance of waking Mindy up that way. And, even though we had to be quiet as we lay there in the dark, tasting and exploring each other's bodies as if for the first time, we felt free together.

On Sunday, I woke up early and made them breakfast. I took Mindy for a walk on the nature trail west of Fairview. Meanwhile, Max stayed in, dealing with the accounts for Fircress Furniture. When we got back, he was waiting in the doorway for us. I studied his face as I undid Mindy's shoes and helped her off with her coat. He looked a little weary and rattled like something was wrong.

"You okay?" I said, looking concerned as Mindy ran inside.

"Yeah, I'm fine," he said, but I could tell he wasn't.

"Whatever it is, let's figure it out together," I replied. I wasn't about to let us get isolated from one another. Not now. Not after how far we had all come in the last few days.

"It's the business reports," he said, sighing. "Actually, not just the business reports. It's everything. The accounts, the bank statements, even the stuff I hear from the factory floor. Nothing makes sense, and the money's not adding up."

I thought suspiciously of Winston. He'd been running the company while Max had taken his time away. I didn't trust him. "Have you spoken to your brother-in-law?" I said.

He shook his head. "He won't talk to me about it. And besides, there's something else..."

"What's that?" I asked.

Max frowned. "A few days ago, your mom called me and asked to speak with me."

I gaped. "What? Why didn't you tell me, Max?"

"I didn't know it was her at the time, and I wouldn't have gone if I'd known. She told me that she'd seen Winston's name on some signs up on the east side of the island. I went to look, and she was right. Winston's bought some land there."

I scowled. "It's not like it's any of my mom's business. She's stirring up trouble, Max. It's what she does."

"Even if that's true..." Max replied, "...it doesn't change the fact that he has acquired that land. Land we hoped would be protected by the federal government and turned into a nature reserve. Somewhere we couldn't build on or develop in any way."

"That sounds nice, I guess," I said. "God knows Mom would love that. She's a huge fan of keeping things wild around here. When I was little, we'd get dragged off to all kinds of PTA meetings. She threw a fit whenever someone wanted to build another parking lot near Mount Criker."

Max nodded. "Anyway, I confronted Winston about it. And he was pretty cagey."

"You really think he has plans for that side of the island?"

"I don't know." Max's face was grim. I could see that he was confused and hurt. "I don't know why he'd do that. Winnie loved this place. She wouldn't have been able to bear seeing it..."

I put my hand on his strong shoulder and squeezed it. He smiled, and the darkness passed over his face.

"Anyway, I need to find out what's really going on. And not knowing is killing me. And, then, there's Trevor."

I nodded. An uneasy silence passed between us. We both knew what Trevor's suspicions really were. But what did that have to do with Max's books? It was a huge mess. We might have spent the perfect weekend together, but things beyond Fairview's tall hedges and wooded driveway were far from perfect.

"Tell you what. This little girl right here..." I gestured to Mindy, who was busy scrabbling around in the kitchen for her bag, "...is pretty hungry. And I think some time with her daddy would be just the trick for both of you. How's that sound?"

Max smiled. "Sounds pretty good. Where are you going, Sophie?"

I smiled. "I'll take out the Jeep, I guess. Go for a drive. See you guys later?"

Max nodded and took Mindy's hand as I left the house, shutting the heavy oak front door behind me.

It had started raining by the time I pulled Max's Jeep out of the driveway and started into town. I don't know why, but something was drawing me to the road that made its way out of town and into the southern end of the island. It had been close to a month and a half since I first touched down at Criker's Isle, but I couldn't believe what had happened between Max and me in that time.

I couldn't deny that my feelings for him had grown now. He wasn't just an incredible businessman; he was a wonderful father, kind and gentle with Mindy. And with each day we spent together, he proved that he cared for me more and more.

As I made my way out, past Bushey's and the side road leading up the airstrip, I realized I'd gone there to see where the accident had happened. Was it a morbid curiosity that had drawn me there, or did I just want to understand more about Max? I wasn't sure. Perhaps I just wanted to see it. Trevor's accusations still lay unspoken between Max and me. Perhaps I thought that seeing the place would help me understand, help me support the man whose presence gave me peace, who I couldn't stop thinking about.

As I drove up the road, I saw it and pulled the car over. They'd now put a barrier on the side of the road as it rounded the north side of the hill. There, a sheer drop led down from the road onto the banks of a river that ran through the ravine. I looked at the trickling stream at the bottom, which was running stronger now than the sea.

I looked at the flat plate of rock that hung off the side of the road. I guess the car must have aquaplaned in the rain, sliding off the rock and rolling down. I thought it must have fallen at least sixty feet, and I shuddered to think of Max in there, what it must have been like. Three years on, you could still see the scattered scree from the impact. The car had landed against a series of boulders at the base of the hill, flattening the ground there. I looked at it for a long time, confused. How could Max have been going so fast up the hill in the rain to head over the edge? It didn't make sense. I guess these things never do. But I still realized why Trevor felt the way he did about it. Perhaps he did need my help after all...

But then, I heard the blip of a police siren behind me and turned as I saw Derrick's car slowing down on the side of the road behind the Jeep.

I was more confident this time. My weekend with Max made me feel like myself again. I wasn't lost on Criker's Isle anymore. I didn't feel like an unwanted presence. He stepped out and shone a flashlight on me.

"Look who's up here, all by her lonesome."

I looked at him. Just the sight of him made me so furious I could hardly speak, but this time I was prepared. I knew what I wanted to say.

"I'm not interested in whatever it is you have to say."

He looked at me. I could see his small, black eyes were angry. He didn't rattle me like he had when we'd first met that day in the driveway at Fairview. And the skinny, ratty boy who'd broken my heart as a child was long gone.

But I was shocked when he smiled, adjusting his wide-brimmed hat a little to wipe off the slick of rain. "Look, Sophie," he said, folding his arms while keeping the torch pointed right in my eyes. "I've had just about enough of trying to be a nice guy and hearing you mouth off to me. I can see that you're still that same dumb kid I rescued from all of this..." he raised his hands, gesturing around him, "...and tried to give a better life."

"Is that how you see it? You really are delusional," I replied, standing my ground. "You were an *abuser*, Derrick. You took my money. You cut me off from my family. I was sixteen when we ran away together. Sixteen. I was a kid. And you took..." I said, my voice trembling with emotion, "...*everything*."

He looked at me. There was no way of brushing this one off. I thought I saw him mutter a curse, but I carried on.

"Because that's what you do, Derrick!" I said, my eyes wide, almost smiling at the pleasure of serving up the truth to him. "*You take things.* You take and take and take until there's nothing left. You never lived up to your promise. You never help anyone around here, in this town. I'm not surprised you managed to lie your way into being the sheriff. And if anyone knew what you really were, they'd run you out of this town, and you'd *never show your cowardly ass here again.*"

The only sound filtering around us was the rain, which drove down hard now, spitting onto the ground, forming deep, wide puddles in the ruts along the road. I listened, watching him stand there, half in shadow by the light of the torch.

"You fucking bitch," he said, muttering it at first, then raising his voice as he took a step forward. "You fucking bitch, I'm going to make sure you regret every word that just came out of your mouth."

He took another few steps towards me. I saw the rain splash off his boots as he came for me, and I knew he was going to kill me or hit me, and there was nothing I could do about it, but as he got close and I felt the mud and the rain on his shoes splatter my jeans, and I saw him raise his hand in the air as if to bring it down, another voice rang out across the road from up the slope.

"STOP!"

We both froze, and I watched Derrick's eyes trace upward to his right. I followed them.

"DON'T YOU TOUCH HER, ASSHOLE!"

We both looked up the slope, and I saw her coming down from amongst the undergrowth. Her hood was above her head, and her shoes and jeans were stained with mud, but I'd recognize her anywhere.

"Get the hell out of town right now, Derrick. Otherwise, we're going right to the mainland and telling them. How'd you fancy a spell in one of your own jail cells?"

Derrick sneered and spat at the ground where Alice stood. "You're lucky mommy came by. I'll be waiting for you, Sophie. You'll regret speaking like that to me."

I didn't know where to look, so I stared at the ground while I heard Derrick get back in his car right away. After a while, after the engine had faded away in the distance and a heavy quiet had settled, I heard my mom's heavy footsteps as she walked towards me in the hissing rain.

Suddenly, I felt arms close around me that I'd never felt before. She clasped me to her, and one of her hands brushed the hair on the back of my head, letting it rest gently on her shoulder. Slowly, I felt my own arms rise involuntarily. I closed them around her and lifted my head, looking into those eyes—eyes which felt like reflections of my own.

"Thanks, mom," I said.

Chapter 18

Max

On Sunday night, I put Mindy to bed and got into my own with a book. I was expecting Sophie to surprise me when she got home, but instead, she must have slept in her own room.

I was a little disappointed Sophie didn't want to spend the night with me but didn't read too much into it. It must be hard for her, not knowing where her responsibilities lay. In her mind, she still had to be Mindy's caregiver. And yet, between us, there now existed a secret, one which had to be hidden at all costs. Mindy couldn't find out—it might undo all the magic Sophie had worked by coming into our lives. And similarly, I couldn't help but think it wasn't the right time to tell anyone. I wanted a chance for people to accept who Sophie was without seeing her as attached to me. I knew folks on the Isle would find lots to like about her.

So, the next day, I waited and gave her some space as she woke up Mindy. I discovered them both on the way out. As Sophie sat Mindy on the stairs and fitted her school boots, I told them both to have a good day.

"Everything alright, Sophie?" I asked her after we'd put Mindy in the car and done up her belt.

"Everything's just fine," she replied. "Had a bit of trouble last night. Can we talk about it later?"

"Sure thing," I said. "Tell you what. How about you come up to my workshop this afternoon? I'll be up there later."

She smiled and nodded. After I'd watched them drive off, I went back into the house. I had an important call to make. The phone number I dialed was one I hadn't used in years.

"Yeah. Grigson here." The voice on the other end of the phone was dry and monotonous.

"Hey, is that Paul? It's Max. Max Fircress."

"Oh. *Max.*" It was almost impossible not to laugh at the drawling, tedious boredom in the voice. "What can I do for you today?"

"It's like this, Paul. I need you to look into my business as it's been for the last two years. As you know, I've taken some time away. When I came back to things a month or so ago, I found a lot of...irregularities."

"Sorry to hear that, Max." Paul Grigson was one of the best business analysts on the East Coast but sounded like he had a permanently blocked nose. I could picture him now, sitting at his gray desk, in his gray office, wearing his suit, which, while probably a classy cut in herringbone, would still be an inevitable gray. "What would you like me to do to help?" he said, his voice weary and hoarse.

"Well, if I send things through to you, are you happy to have a look for me, Grigson? I'll pay a premium if you can complete it within a week. I feel like time might be of the essence here."

Paul Grigson sighed as though this request had utterly crushed his spirit. I knew that, secretly, Paul loved nothing more than to peruse a few thousand pages of Microsoft Excel and could do so with precision and skill.

"Sure thing. Can do. Send it over." Each sentence's inflections drooped downwards at the end, like the ears on a sad basset hound.

"Glad to hear it, Paul. I'll send it all through to you now. Good luck."

"Talk soon, *Max*."

With that, the phone conversation was mercifully concluded.

I looked at my clock and saw that it was 9 am already. After Paul had sent through the usual contract and NDA, I finished my correspondence and decided it was time to head out to the workshop.

I've never been keen on spending money for a guy with over three billion dollars in his bank account. The *Puffin*, my sailboat, was second-hand, and I'd spent a summer fixing it up five years ago. And Fairview had been constructed as efficiently as possible, with almost no wastage. I could have hired contractors to do it, but in the end, most of the work was done by Winnie and me. We liked to do things ourselves. But the workshop was a labor of love for me, and I'd spared no expense.

It was located in an annex at the back of the guesthouse up on the slopes above Fairview. Winston thought the thing was an eyesore and liked to complain about it now and then when he came to stay. "When are you going to tear that thing down?" was his favorite question to ask me. I usually smiled and joked about it, but the truth was, I was never going to get rid of it.

I walked up the hill and went around to the back of the guesthouse, where it stood, a squat plywood building built on a raised deck. I looked through the window of the guesthouse to see if I could spy Winston at work in the office there. I couldn't.

At the back of the workshop was a special lift, converted from industrial equipment, where the various creations therein could be lowered onto the back of a truck or trolley to be taken away. In some ways, it had been the heart of Fircress Furniture. Though in recent years, we've become used to hiring designers and producing new models on the mainland. When I'd first moved here with Winnie, everything the company manufactured was based on prototypes built in the workshop. I wished it could be that way again.

I unlocked the door and entered, the smell of sawdust and varnish filling my nostrils. In a room at the front was a small office, which had been Winnie's while she was alive. The workshop was through the office, a bright, airy space with a wide table at one end for smaller builds. It was flanked by a lathe and a few different worktables. One was kitted out with vices and a bandsaw. A thin sheet of aluminum housed my tools on the wall, hung neatly and carefully on nails and hooks in the metal. Drills, saws, hammers, and nails in neatly labeled bags all sat sadly on the wall, long neglected.

In the center of the room, on a raised dais, was the start of something new, a project I'd begun shortly after Winnie's death and never completed. It was a chair made out of regeneratively forested oak. It was hard to see how the rough dovetail joints and wooden dowel pins which extruded from its arms would ever make a finished project, but now, in my mind's eye, I knew what to do with it.

I started by lifting the chair off its plinth, running my hands lovingly over its wide back and comfortable, chunky arms. I'd been inspired to start it with a picture I had when I was a kid of my dad's living room. Most of our furniture had been made by him, and the chair was intended to have the look and feel of one

I'd seen him make shortly before he passed. Now, even though I was distracted by thoughts of Winston, the company, and Sophie, I knew I was going to finish it, no matter what.

I started out with a simple hammer and chisel and began to gently knock the pattern I had in mind into the top of the chair's back. I wanted a gentle sloping architecture for the chair, which would allow for comfort when the person sitting in it rested their head against the back. But I also wanted it to look elegant, and modern. As I began to work, slowly and patiently setting my weight against the wood, I saw the pencil etchings I'd placed in the chair, undamaged by time. They showed the pattern and detail I was going to carve into the thing, slowly working away to reveal a gentle, sloping arch filled with etched reliefs of flowers and trees.

Within no time at all, sawdust and wood chippings littered the floor. I stopped, wanting to work just as diligently and orderly as I remembered my dad working when I was a kid. I stopped and swept up, depositing the shavings into a bin I kept by the door of the workshop. Everything could be used, every little bit recycled. I didn't want to waste an inch of the precious wood that had been grown for this particular chair.

Hours passed as I worked on the chair. I hardly even noticed when, down below, I heard the Jeep pull up. And I didn't even notice when Sophie opened the door to the workshop and walked in slowly, gingerly.

Eventually, I turned around to get a better angle with my chisel and stood up. She was leaning in the doorway with a strange smile playing on her lips.

"Having fun?" she said. I smiled and nodded, lifting the chair and depositing it on its legs. I'd almost finished on the back now— all that would be left was to carve a bit more detail tomorrow, then finish the legs. Finally, I'd work to scoop out some more wood from the seat of the chair, curving it a little and completing the look I had in mind.

"It's not quite there yet, but it's going to be a real beauty when I've finished," I said, walking over to the wall and replacing my tools gently. "Almost as beautiful as you, that is."

She giggled and walked across the hall to me. "I took you up on your offer to come see you up here. Hope you're not too tired," she said as she threw her arms around me. I took her by the waist, and we kissed while one of her hands found its way into the stubble on my chin and scratched it, tender and loving.

"I'll never get tired of you," I said. The pride I felt in my work now transferred to the pride I felt in having such a gorgeous woman in my arms, and I kissed her deeply again, pulling her close, wanting to feel her body against me again. "Where were you last night, mystery girl?"

She pulled her hair back, looping an errant strand around her ear. I loved the way her hair got loose. "It's a long story, but I have a bit of a favor to ask."

"What's that?" I said, eager to give her anything she wanted.

"Well, I kind of ran into my mom yesterday..." she said. "And she was wondering if...if we'd like to come for dinner at the house this Friday."

"Oh yeah?" I said. "Is...is your whole family going to be there?"

She shrugged her shoulders, those gorgeous, delicate narrow shoulders which only drew my eyes to her bosom more easily. "Not sure. It's the day of Mindy's trip to the Science Museum on the mainland. She won't be back until eight. Will you come, Max? It would mean a lot. You've been so good to us...to me, especially."

I knew it wasn't just out of gratitude that she was inviting me. Sophie was asking for my support more than anything else. And as much as I held trepidation in my heart about seeing Trevor, and Belinda, again, I knew I'd do anything for her then. "Whatever you want, sweetheart," I cooed, and she smiled, reaching up and kissing my cheeks and neck.

"I have half an hour before I need to fetch Mindy," she said.

"Half an hour it is, then," I said and pulled her back until I was sitting on the long desk of the workshop with her in my lap.

She kissed me while I frantically pulled at the buttons of her shirt. It was an autumnal blouse, mustardy in color and made of soft, thick satin. Gradually, I eased her onto the table until she lay there in front of me, soft, and inviting, her skirt rucked up above her knees to reveal that she wasn't wearing anything beneath her pantyhose.

I growled, the sight sending shivers down my spine. "You go out like that today?"

She smiled. "Actually..." she said coquettishly, "...I took them off before I came up here. Figured you'd like it."

"Well, you know what I think?" I said as I cradled her thighs, massaging them gently, making her whimper. "I think you must be a very badly behaved young woman."

She smiled at that. Then, a little petulantly, she replied, "Show me."

I was only too happy to oblige.

It was the work of a moment to ease off her panties, pulling them down until they were around her ankles. I climbed onto the desk beside her, gently placing a hand between her legs. As Sophie moaned, I spread the lips of her pussy with my hand while the other found its way into her hair. I'd never been with someone whose body felt so attuned to mine, who anticipated every movement I made—and loved it.

But I was too desperate now and had to have her. She felt so light in my hands that it was easy to turn her onto her front, and now I unzipped my pants, letting my erect cock slide in between her legs, making moans and sounds of delight escape from her throat as she kneeled before me, spreading her legs, straining to open for me. I gave her a playful smack on the rear, and she gasped happily.

"You gonna play around all day, or are you going to give me what I want?" said Sophie.

I was desperate to be inside her again, but I decided to see how wild she could be driven. I pushed my cock up against her clit, rubbing it there for a few moments, reveling in her squeals of pleasure.

"What do you want me to do?" I heard myself say, made ravenous and animalistic by the feeling of her naked skin against mine. I saw she'd slipped a hand inside her blouse and was cupping one of her perky little breasts, feeling it, exposing her desire to me.

"I want you to fuck me," she said.

"Like this?" I pressed the head of my now fully erect dick against her center and felt her knees practically buckle.

"Yes, yes, just like that. Fuck me, Max."

I pushed deep inside her, and she yelped before applying pressure on her hands and pushing herself onto me. It was hard to tell who was in control. Sophie wanted me so much that she was practically having me all by herself. Each of us was in competition to see who could more fiercely possess the other, and I gripped her shoulders and began to screw her with hard, slow thrusts that rocked her from the inside.

"Deeper...deeper," Sophie cried as I fucked her passionately. I gathered her hair in one hand, making sure to lock my fist close to her scalp, where it wouldn't hurt but would feel deliciously possessive and controlling. I wanted her to know how she raised those feelings in me.

I fucked her faster, uncontrollably, and she bucked and shuddered. The table rocked a little, and I saw her slide her arms down and put her head among a pile of creased blueprints. "Yes, Max...yes...harder, please, please, please."

I didn't disappoint and kept pounding harder and harder while Sophie's knuckles grew white as she moaned into the surface of the desk. I felt myself roar as I gave way, exploding inside her, and Sophie came at the same time, climaxing and moaning, as she lifted her head up and buried me deep inside her while I felt my pulsing cock release.

We stayed there for a while before I pulled out, watching a trickle of semen run down the inside of her thigh. Sophie collapsed onto the table, rolled onto her back, and kicked up her legs in the air.

"God, that was incredible," she said. I sat on the desk beside her, gently stroking her hair and bending down to kiss her sweaty cheeks.

After she'd cleaned herself up, I helped her off, lovingly adjusting her blouse and skirt, so it wouldn't look like she'd just enjoyed a quickie when she turned up at the school gates. I brushed sawdust off her shoulders. It was one of the most exciting things that had ever happened to me, and before she left, I couldn't help but grasp her in my arms again and whisper, "You're mine," into her left ear. She blew a kiss as she left the workshop while I slumped in the chair I'd been carving that morning, feeling like the luckiest man in the world.

Chapter 19

Sophie

The days that week passed quickly. I was apprehensive about seeing my family for dinner on Friday, but with Max, I could lose myself and enjoy the time spent with him. During the days while Mindy was at school, we met in secret, often while he was in his workshop or the house. We took walks together and shared our meals. I knew what the whole town would say when they found out about us, but I didn't care. I was starting to realize just how deep my feelings for Max went, how they skirted all the treacherous roads in my soul that had led me to fall under Derrick's spell, to be alone and miserable for years.

Max was healing me day by day, showing me that I could put my trust in him to catch me when I fell. Whatever we did, we did it together.

During the day, when time allowed, we'd go to bed together, and I'd feel his hands cradle, soothe, and make me whole again. I'd trace the scar on his chest and kiss it gently. It had been a deep wound and still left a strip of creased tissue from his right pectoral to his left abdomen. But it was part of him, and I accepted it and cherished it, just like I cherished Max.

When Friday finally came, I realized the butterflies that had been in my stomach all week hadn't just been there on Max's account. I was nervous about seeing them again; Belinda, my mom, my dad, and Trevor. Having us all in a room again would be a strange experience.

After I took Mindy to school and came back to the house, I sat with Max and read for a while as he worked. Mindy was taking the ferry that morning to the mainland, where the kids were going to see the Science Museum. I made Mrs. Deleaney put me on speed dial in case there were any problems, but the truth was, I was calm about Mindy and excited for her. A few weeks ago, no one could have imagined her being in the right headspace to go to the mainland or be around kids her age so far from the security of Fairtown Elementary School. But she'd rapidly transformed, shedding her former preoccupations and distance. There was warmth in her eyes now and boundless energy that made her a handful to take care of at times.

Just like a kid ought to be, I thought.

She was perfect, and I told her so. I let her hug me now when she said goodbye and hello. I didn't give a damn what anyone else thought. Mindy hadn't called me *Mommy* again since that night in the restaurant. Was it possible it had just been a slip of the tongue? I hoped so.

When night started to fall, Max and I drove off. I guess it must have been about 5.30 pm. My old house, the house I'd grown up in, was only a short drive away.

"You already know where it is?" I asked Max as we wound around the country lanes, and up the hill to the village.

"I know where most places are around here..." he replied, "...but I actually paid a visit to your dad a few weeks ago."

He explained to me he'd wanted to ask them to reach out to

me. "He must really respect you," I said. "That's amazing."

Max smiled bashfully, but a crease in his brow gave away the fact that he was feeling more than a little nervous about seeing them.

"Trevor's gonna be there, isn't he?" I nodded. Max spoke again. "He's going to want to talk about what happened to Winnie."

I didn't know what to say about that. Despite how close we'd grown in such a short time, there were still things that seemed off-limits with Max. Winnie was one of them. I couldn't imagine how it felt to have someone else in his arms in the house he'd built for her. Sometimes I felt enormously guilty, as though I was an imposter in Winnie's shoes. Other times I was able to think more clearly, and at those moments, I knew that the way he felt about me was completely different, that the relationship forming between us couldn't be understood in comparison to his years with Winnie.

"He might want to, but you don't have to," I replied. "You only ever need to talk about what you're comfortable with."

We pulled up at the house. I was astonished to see how little it had changed. The same little flowerbeds and potted plants sat outside. They'd even kept the old water pump by the side of the house, in which Trevor and I had played when we were kids.

Max looked over as he switched off the engine. He could see my shoulders were tense and reached out a reassuring hand. "I'll be right behind you," he said.

But the truth was, he looked nervous too.

When my dad saw me on the doorstep, he stepped over awkwardly and embraced me. It was a far cry from the cold greeting I'd received at the airport. I felt the merest hint of anger that he'd let my mom keep him from hugging his own daughter for so long but suppressed it. Today was about forgiveness, after all.

As we came into the kitchen, I saw my mom busy in front of a row of pots and pans, lit by the glaring yellow light of a 100-watt bulb. "I was going to make shepherd's pie," she said. "Turns out we're having beef mince and mashed potatoes."

I wanted to laugh at that but forced a smile instead. "Sounds great, mom." My mother had never been good in the kitchen. I looked around at the house, a house in which I hadn't set foot in fourteen years. It looked much the same as I remembered, but my parents didn't. My dad looked older, tired now, with most of his hair gone and what was left of it turned gray. My mom still looked just as strong as she did when I knew her, but her face was carved with lines. She'd finally shed her outer layer of rainproof clothing and was dressed in a comfortable wool-knit jumper and a pair of jeans. She still wore her shoes inside the house, though.

"Trevor will be back soon," said my mom. "Belinda too," she added, a little more sharply.

Out of the corner of my eye, I saw Max look worried again.

"Doesn't Belinda have her own place?" I asked. I didn't know how things would go with us.

When I'd left Criker's Isle with Derrick all those years ago, Belinda had been the angriest about it. I guess to her, I was the irresponsible middle child, free from responsibility but not as deserving of love and warmth like my younger brother, Trevor. To me, she'd always be the haughty older sister, deciding what was in my best interests before I'd had a chance.

Before my mom could answer for Belinda, Trevor arrived, wiping his boots on the mat. He hugged me and shook Max's hand enthusiastically, beaming. "Man, I'm so glad you guys could make it!" he said. "It's been a long day. Derrick's out of town."

"Yeah. She knows," said my mom, turning around and giving

me the eye. Since that night on the road up by the airstrip, we hadn't seen Derrick. He'd gone off-island—he didn't give much of an explanation to anyone—leaving Trevor in charge for a few days. It was crazy to think that my younger brother was responsible for the entire population of the island, which wasn't much, to be honest. Last I checked, we were about 500 residents, give or take a few tourists visiting before winter. Two other deputies recently joined, but as the acting sheriff of Fairtown, Trevor was responsible for things while Derrick was away. Mom and I knew why Derrick was gone—her ambush had provided a witness to his threats and intimidation. Finally, there was someone else who could back me up if Max and I ever had to prove what we knew—that Derrick had been harassing and intimidating me since I first set foot back on Criker's Isle. At any rate, we knew he wouldn't be back for a while.

We sat and talked for a while as my mom started to set down plates. I tried to help, but she was insistent on doing everything herself.

"How's Mindy getting along?" my dad asked, breaking an uneasy silence.

Max whistled a little through his teeth. I felt a little embarrassed to see him here. We'd decided not to tell anyone about us, but I felt like it must have been glaringly obvious.

"She's doing just fine..." he said, "...thanks to Sophie here."

"And you're happy with the job she's doing?" my mom said. I noted a hint of suspicion in her voice. Even though we'd said little to one another, it already felt like she was apologizing for me to Max. I bristled at her tone but held my tongue.

"Very happy," Max replied. "You must be very proud of her."

"We'd have been prouder if she'd let us know what she was doing," my mom answered.

"*Mom*," I hissed. Now wasn't the time to air our grievances, not in front of Max.

Tension was already brewing in the tiny kitchen, but Trevor defused it quickly. His eyes were full of hope as he leaned in.

"Actually, I had to speak to Mrs. Deleaney the other day about a kid at the school. She mentioned how well Mindy's been doing. She's pretty impressed with her. Says she has the makings of an artist."

My mom raised an eyebrow as she sat down and began to fix our plates. She served my dad first, then Max. "Is that right? Sophie was always keen on drawing when she was Mindy's age. Weren't you, Sophie?"

"She was also keen on staying out late and getting into trouble, as far as I remember," said a voice from the kitchen doorway.

It was Belinda. She'd snuck in without any of us hearing her.

An uneasy silence settled over the table as my dad began to eat.

Belinda took a seat next to Max. She started to serve herself.

"Well, Sophie certainly isn't staying out late anymore," Max replied cordially. "In fact, she's pretty devoted to Mindy. Doesn't go anywhere without knowing where my daughter is."

"Not what I heard," said Belinda as she took a bite of her food. "Mom, this is dreadful."

My mother sighed and pushed her food away. "Not like you to be late for dinner, Belinda."

"We're not here to discuss my teenage growing pains, Bee," I said coldly. I could feel the hairs on the back of my neck beginning to rise.

"No, we're not," added my mom. "We're all here because we

miss Sophie. We want her back in our lives, Max. And we're grateful to you for making that happen."

Max shrugged. "Sophie's here because she wants to be here. Isn't that right, Sophie?" He looked at me as he said the words and gave me an encouraging smile.

I nodded.

Belinda rolled her eyes. She could abide my mom standing up for me, but it seemed she had a problem when Max did it.

Why is that?

She eyed our parents as she continued to eat. "Doesn't it bother you..." she said slowly, after taking another bite of her food, "...that she hasn't spoken to either of you since she arrived? And now, all of a sudden, we're here, playing happy families?"

"Bee." This time it was Trevor who spoke. I could see the hurt on his face. He'd clearly hoped this would be an occasion for us to make peace. His voice was tense. This wasn't the first time he'd been present for an argument between us.

"Doesn't it bother you..." I said calmly, "...that everyone here's ready to forgive me, except for you? That you're still holding onto the past like it could change anything?"

Belinda scoffed. "Seems to me that nothing's changed, Sophie. I heard you were hanging out at The Red Rod the other night. Heard that you were talking to Derrick."

Trevor looked confused. "Is that true, Sophie?"

"I can't stop him from talking to me, Trevor. I'm just lucky Max was there, too, to stop us fighting. You conveniently left that part out, didn't you, Bee?"

"That man..." Alice said, "...has caused more harm to this family than Sophie ever did. And I think we'd do well to remember that. Whatever the reason for him bothering you, we're all behind you."

"Speak for yourself," said Belinda.

"ENOUGH." I didn't mean to shout, but I did. "Let's be honest, Belinda. It's not Derrick or my past that bothers you so much, is it?"

"What's that supposed to mean?" Belinda shot back while an ugly look of resentment flooded her face.

"Guys, please," whispered Trevor. My dad said nothing, but he'd put his fork down.

"I mean..." I said, "...that if you're angry about me living at Fairview, you should just come out and say it."

"I'm angry that you're looking after a little girl," said Belinda. "I'm angry that you're walking around here pretending to be responsible when the truth is that you were still shacked up with Derrick on the mainland ten years ago. After you broke mom's heart by running out in the first place."

"You'd better settle down, Bee." My mom's voice was hard like iron. Her eyes had that soft glow about them, a glow I remembered all too well from family arguments in the old days.

"I won't *settle down*," said Belinda petulantly. "Not when the rumor is that these two are having some kind of sordid affair while Mindy goes neglected—"

"Neglected?" I said, throat tightening. "You're a joke, Bee."

"Piss off, Sophie. No one wanted you back here in the first place."

"*BELINDA!*" My mom was furious now. "Calm down, or else..."

But Belinda had already got up to leave.

***

I sat outside on the porch for a while to calm down. My shoulders were still shaking by the time Max came out to get me. He sat down beside me, and I rested my head on his shoulder. Inside, I could hear the clatter of plates as my mom cleaned up the remains of our disastrous dinner.

"I'm so sorry," he said. "Belinda can be—"

"A titanic bitch?" I finished for him, and he laughed a single, mirthless chuckle.

"Yeah. I guess. But I still believe her heart's in the right place."

"Well, when you figure out where that place is, make sure you tell me."

He sighed. I looked up and studied his face. I could tell there was something he wanted to tell me but didn't know what it was. Was Max hiding something?

He looked at his shoes but said nothing. "Look. I know you don't want to go back in there, but I feel I owe it to you to stick around for a bit. They barely know me, and even if it can't be that way now, I want them to know they can rely on me. On us. We're not going anywhere. You're not going anywhere, Sophie. And it's important that I get to know them. For the future."

"You're amazing," I said. "Even after all this, you're still trying to help me sort out this messed-up family situation."

"It's the least I can do. And, if you want to talk about messed-up family situations..."

He didn't need to finish that sentence.

"I need to pick up Mindy," I said, wiping a tear from my eye. "The ferry's coming in soon."

Max nodded. "Trevor said he's happy to give me a lift. You get

Mindy and take her back to the house. How's that sound?"

I nodded. "Sounds good."

He stood up and kissed my head. "I'll see you later."

Max went back inside. I heard his voice talking, low and confident. It was clear they liked him a lot. One day, I knew I'd be proud to tell them what Max and I shared, what we shared with Mindy together. But right now, it was too confusing for me to deal with. I focused my mind on Mindy. She'd had a big day and was going to need my full attention.

After sitting there on the porch for a little while, I pulled myself together and got up. I walked over to Max's Jeep, parked out on the driveway. But when I got there, I heard hushed voices, whispering and agitated.

I pricked up my ears and turned. Whoever was talking, they were behind the house on the back porch.

I listened closely. Slowly, I backed away from the Jeep and went around to the side wall of the house. When we were kids, Trevor and I had hidden there for hours at a time, listening to my parents talking in the garden or making fun of Belinda's endless phone calls to her friends. I crouched. I could hear Max's voice and...Belinda's? They were talking, and I felt a pang of jealousy run through me and a cold feeling of fear in my chest while they stood arguing behind the house.

"Is it true, Max? Is it? Because if it is, I—"

"It's none of your business, Belinda. Nothing about my life has ever been your business."

"You're such a hypocrite. You always were."

"I'm here today for Sophie. Not for anything else. Do you understand that?"

"You're here because she's made you come here. She manipulated you. And it isn't fair. It isn't fair how you'll do anything for her, and—"

"And what, Belinda?" Max sounded mad. In fact, he didn't sound like himself at all. Whatever they were talking about, it was something I wasn't party to. Why were they fighting? And why did they sound so damn familiar with one another?

"You only had to give it a chance. Was that too much to ask?"

"Belinda, if you insist on going down this path after I've made myself clear, I can't help you."

"But Max...you can't just..."

Belinda knew something about Max, something she wasn't prepared to let on in front of us. And Max knew something too. Something he was keeping from me.

"Belinda, I won't do this with you..."

I backed away, Max's voice fading into the background. My hands were shaking so hard, I was afraid they could hear the jangle of the car keys in my hand.

Could I have been right in thinking that Bee was jealous of me being in Fairview? Of me and Max? How could I have been so blind?

It was a lot to unpack.

I can't do this. Mindy needs me.

Hurt, ashamed, and thoroughly afraid, I left them to it and got in the Jeep. I didn't have the heart to confront them. Or to ask Max what was going on between him and Belinda.

I was too afraid of what the truth might be.

Chapter 20

Max

I felt a quiet sense of foreboding in the pit of my stomach as Trevor drove me home that night in his squad car. The fight with Belinda had rattled me. Luckily, I didn't think Sophie would have heard us. I'd worked too hard to gain her trust to compromise it now. But I felt the heaviness of that and the heaviness of Trevor's thoughts as we made our way back to the house, like the air before a thunderstorm. I was so lost in my own troubles I didn't notice when Trevor pulled us quietly into a layby and turned the engine off.

"Max, I respect you too much to lie. And after tonight, seeing what resentments and unspoken things can do to a family, it's only fair that I tell you what's been on my mind lately."

I sighed and clenched my fists, closing my eyes and pushing my head back into the seat. The fight at Sophie's family's house had left me with a headache, and I rubbed my chest, where the scar was burning away like a bright fire.

"You'd better tell me what you have to say, Trevor," I said. "Before I stop you."

He took a deep breath and pinched his brow. When Winnie and I had first come to the island, I'd seen Trevor around a few times. Back then, he was just one of the neighborhood kids, pumping gas or working at one of the convenience stores to make a few extra bucks. But I'd seen the change in him when he came back from police training on the mainland. He was taller and more athletic. Now I had to acknowledge that the boy I'd seen around town seven years ago was a man now. And it looked like he was carrying the weight of the world on his shoulders.

"Before, when we talked, I said that Derrick's report was sketchy. Well, I was right. In fact, the one stored in our records isn't even the actual report."

I looked at him, trying to hide the expression on my face. He was determined to rip the bandage off a wound I'd sustained years ago. Part of me wanted to tell him to stop, but another part wanted him to spill the truth more quickly.

"Derrick's covered something up. I don't know what, and I don't know how. But there was some detail about the accident, about your wife's death, that he wanted to hide. The real notes are hidden. And they contain information...information about the car, the injuries you both sustained, and the road conditions...that Derrick doesn't want anyone else in the sheriff's office to know. Understand?"

I nodded.

Trevor searched my face for an answer, but he wasn't going to find one there. "Max, I hate to ask about this. God knows you've suffered enough prodding and poking about that night. But..."

He paused. "Go on," I whispered.

He looked into my eyes. "I need you to tell me what happened."

***

"Oh, Lord. Look at the time, Max. We're gonna be late."

"I'm working on it, hon. Just...relax. We'll get there when we get there."

Winnie picked up her cell phone and dialed back to Fairview. Outside, the rain hammered against the car window, and I saw the lights of Fairtown twinkling in the rearview mirror. *"Trust our luck to hold a gala dinner on the night of the worst storm in fifteen years."*

I could hear my wife's cell phone ringing as she waited for someone to pick it up, pulling a strand of her long, black hair behind her ear. *"Hi? Patricia? Is that you?"*

A voice on the other end mumbled something I couldn't hear.

"Well, Winston be damned. If he's not coming, he's not coming. I just need to know if Mindy's going to be alright if we have to spend the night on the mainland. No chance of getting a ferry back in this weather. They're already canceled."

Again, I heard a nervous voice, young and worried, talk back.

"Alright. I'll call you later and let you know." Winnie put the phone down.

"She's such a lovely girl, but my goodness, she worries," said Winnie after a while. A peal of thunder crackled and broke the sky open. The sun was down now, and the rain began to hammer on the windscreen in thick, black globules.

"There's no way they're going to run a flight in this weather," I said.

"That's not an option, Max. We promised we'd try to get there. Can you imagine what the board of directors will say if we miss our own charity event?"

I smiled grimly. *"I'll do my best, captain. I will."*

I could tell something else was on her mind as we sped past Bushey's diner. Outside I could see an unhappy couple standing in raincoats at the door. The lights were on, but no one was in.

"Christ. Even the diner's closed tonight. There's no way we're flying, Winnie."

"I'll be the judge of that, thank you."

I looked at her. I could tell something was bothering her from the tense note in her voice. I took my foot off the accelerator as we began to round the hill. I couldn't risk driving fast in this weather.

"You okay, Win? I know when you're upset about something."

She turned to look at me, and I thought I saw her open her mouth in the wing mirror as I checked behind us. No one was on the road. She must have thought better of what she was about to say next and promptly tried to change the subject.

"Was that a police car I saw by Bushey's? You don't think anything happened up there, do you?"

"Win," I replied, smirking. Even if she didn't realize it, the secret was written on her face. *"Whatever it is, you can tell me."*

*"Oh, Winston and I fought this afternoon, if you **must** know,"* she said. I braced myself for a tide of expletives. I'd never met two siblings more at odds.

"About what?" I said. We were almost there.

"I'll tell you about it later. But Max..." she said, *"...I don't want you to—"*

There was a bang and a jolt like we'd just run over something.

"What the—" I said as rain splattered the screen. I took my foot off the accelerator and hit the brakes.

The car didn't want to give. It was like the wheels had frozen.

"*Max?*" said Winnie nervously as we skated towards the edge. I watched in front of me as the hood of the car began to swing slowly, awfully towards the left, like a pendulum on a grandfather clock. We were skidding down the hilltop now towards a bend in the road.

"*MAX!*" screamed Winnie, and then all of a sudden, we were falling, falling for what seemed like forever, as the weight of the car pulled us round and around.

The last thing I saw was her face, wide-eyed and frightened, before the loudest noise I'd ever heard ran straight through me and sent me spinning, spinning onwards.

Into darkness.

***

Trevor and I sat for a long time in the squad car once I'd finished talking. My shoulders were shaking slowly. It had been the first time since the accident that I spoke to anyone about what happened in vivid detail. I wanted to sob and cry, but it was like I'd forgotten how.

"It wasn't an accident, was it?" I said slowly, quietly.

Trevor shook his head. "Doesn't sound like it to me. If what you've told me is true."

"It is," I said. "God knows I've thought about that night enough. What happened, Trevor?"

From the way his eyes flickered and flitted on the road behind him, I could see he already had suspicions. Was he nervous about something?

"I don't know yet," said Trevor. "But I promise I'll get to the bottom of it."

He started the engine again, and we began to drive up the road. "You're a good man," I said. "Definitely got my vote for sheriff next time there's an election."

Trevor looked ashamed. "I think I'd better sort out my own household before I set my mind to anyone else's affairs. Hey, can I ask you something?"

"Sure," I said, steeling myself for more questions about the accident.

"How long have you and my sister been together?"

I was shocked.

"Trevor, I..."

He laughed. "Relax, Max. I'm over the moon for you. Don't know if my parents have twigged yet. Belinda's going to freak out. But Derrick wasn't wrong, was he? Even if he is an asshole. You guys *are* an item."

I wanted to apologize, and I didn't even know why. "She doesn't want to tell anyone," I said. "Can you please help us keep it a secret?"

"Oh, sure," he said. "Sure, hell, I wouldn't tell a soul. You know how it is. Small town and all that. I...I couldn't be happier, Max. I really couldn't. I just want everything to be straight, you know? It must be tricky, what with her looking after your kid and all."

I nodded. "We're taking it slow," I said. "Well, trying. Mindy can't...that wouldn't be fair, you understand?"

"I do. But, Max. I've gotta ask. What's going on with Belinda?"

"Belinda?" I said, trying to sound as innocent as possible.

Trevor sighed and leaned back in his seat. In the distance, the lights of Fairview were on. I relaxed, happy that Sophie and Mindy would be there to meet me when we arrived.

"We've all known she was sweet on you from the day you arrived. Lord, when you and Mrs. Fircress used to be a bit more involved with the school and everything, she couldn't stop talking about you. Is that what's going on? Is it jealousy?"

I said nothing, and now Trevor, like the bloodhound he was, smelled my cowardice, the lie forming on my lips. I looked out of the window and told him the truth.

"You're gonna hate me for this."

He said nothing. I carried on talking.

"After Winnie died, Trevor...I was hopeless. Mindy was away with relatives for a bit. I was up here by myself. I just...I just went crazy. I was drinking like a fish."

I thought I heard Trevor mutter something, but I couldn't make out what he had said. So I carried on speaking. I think I was hoping he'd stop and throw me out of the car, but he didn't.

"I met Belinda at The Red Rod one night and...well, we kissed. She kissed me. I was drunk. I was stupid and didn't know what I was thinking, putting myself in that situation. It wasn't fair on anyone. Especially her."

We were almost in the driveway of Fairview now.

"And, afterward, she kept...talking to me. Kept following me around and kept speaking to Mindy like...like something more was going to come of it. Nothing did, nothing ever did, I swear. It was a stupid, drunken kiss, and I regret it. I thought she did too. I thought we'd agreed to forget about it."

"Whatever you think you agreed..." Trevor said quietly, "...it's not what she agreed to."

I shook my head. "No, it's not. And Sophie can never find out. She'd hate me. You must hate me already. I mean, Jesus Christ, these are your sisters."

Trevor stopped the squad car. We were at the bottom of the driveway now, but it was clear we were going no further. He folded both his arms on the steering wheel and rested his chin on them.

"I don't hate you, Max. God knows no one will ever understand what you went through. And I know how Belinda can be like. It's a shame. If she was sweet on you before that happened, then...well, it's a small town. Not many nice guys like you around, right?"

I balled my fists. I wanted to beat my hands against my head. I felt like a lot of things right now, but a nice guy wasn't one of them.

"But..." said Trevor, "...you do have to tell Sophie. I owe you an honest explanation for why your wife died, Max—"

"You don't owe me that—" I butted in, but he carried on talking.

"—But you owe Sophie an explanation for why things are the way they are with her sister," finished Trevor. "You know that."

He was right. I said nothing else but got out of the car. The house looked so lonely with its lights on in the dark.

Chapter 21

Sophie

I decided to take Mindy to the beach for a walk the next day. Last night, I'd waited for Max to come home, but I didn't feel like talking when he finally arrived. I sat in my room, wondering if he'd come to speak to me. He didn't.

Mindy and I sat together on the beach, watching the waves crash in.

"What did you see at the Science Museum?" I asked, hoping she'd tell me to take my mind off things. But Mindy didn't say anything. She stayed there staring at the waves.

"Mindy? Won't you tell me?" My eyes scanned her face. It was like her old self had returned, distant and sullen. "Was everything okay yesterday? At the ferry, Mrs. Deleaney said you'd been very good..."

Mindy folded her arms. "You're *sad*," she said.

I was taken aback by that and couldn't really think what to say in response. "I...I...I am not."

"Are too," said Mindy, and then she giggled.

I couldn't help but smile. Mindy was wise beyond her years, I guess. She didn't feel like talking to me because she didn't feel like sharing her feelings with anyone who was hiding theirs. I thought about that as I looked up the dunes at Fairview in the distance. I guess I could relate.

"Sophie?" said Mindy.

"Yes, honey?" I replied. I loved it when she called me by my name.

"I...I like you," she said.

I smiled, and my cheeks turned a bright shade of pink. "I like you too, butterscotch," I replied. I can't remember why that nickname had stuck. It just had.

Mindy was quiet for a while. She scraped a shell resting on the shore with one foot. "One day, will you go away? When I'm big?"

"I...don't know, sweetheart. Your daddy pays me to look after you, see. I work for him. You won't need me when you're older. You'll be independent and—"

But she already had her arms around me; her curls were buried in my stomach, and it felt heartbreaking to go on, to tell her that, in the grand scheme of things, I was nothing yet, and even if I did want to be more, even if I did want to take care of her forever, I could never be what Winnie had been to her. My heart had been stolen twice since I came back to Criker's Isle. I could see that now.

"I wish you could be here forever," she said, and I affectionately stroked her curls.

"Me too, sweetheart. Let's hope, huh?"

I brought her home before midday. Max must have been working; he was wearing that sexy pair of reading glasses he always put on and came straight to the door when he heard us come back. I was immediately aflame for him but kept my feelings under control.

"Did Trevor talk to you?" I asked.

He nodded. Max looked tired and in pain. Once Mindy had gone up to her room, I put my hands on his cheeks and kissed his forehead. But he seemed reticent to hold me, to show me his affection. I chalked it up to the presence of his daughter nearby and pulled away.

"He did. Says there's some stuff in Derrick's office that he wants to see. Suppose there's even less chance of finding it now Derrick's gone to the mainland."

I nodded, trying to look like I wasn't already forming a plan.

"Mind if I take the Jeep into town?"

"Sure," he said. "Can...can we talk later?"

"Yeah. Of course we can," I said, smiling.

Max went up to Mindy's room to get her changed. I rebuttoned my coat and headed out.

***

The sheriff's office was in Fairtown, and as I drove there, I had a wild feeling of excitement. I didn't have a plan, much less an idea of how I was going to find the file Trevor was after, but I knew I had to do it. Once I had that, things could get back to normal, or at least as normal as they could be.

I parked on the street, opposite the office. There weren't any squad cars outside. The office was a gray stucco building on one story adjoining a doctor's office. As I turned off the engine, I leaned back in the seat of the Jeep and watched the windows for any signs of life.

The Billionaire's Nanny

There was nothing. Trevor must have been out; if one of the other deputies was in town that day, they weren't there.

I stayed there for a while, ducking or shielding my face when a car drove past.

I bet they haven't even locked it, a voice said from within me.

Time to find out.

Quickly, I got out of the car and walked towards the front door. I put my hand on it, and, to my surprise, it opened.

"You guys need to be a little more security-conscious," I murmured.

Inside there was a plastic desk where a receptionist usually sat on weekdays. The cells were at the back of the building. I only knew that because once, when Derrick and I first started dating, he'd been picked up and left to sit in the drunk tank overnight. My mom had a lot to say about that.

I checked the door to my left. I saw a few sofas, a water cooler, and a kitchenette with a coffee machine through the glass. It was clearly a breakroom of some kind. On the right was a large, open-plan space with a pair of desks, on top of which sat two enormous, old computers. I opened it and walked through.

Derrick's office was in an enclosed space, one of those old-time offices with frosted glass and darkly varnished, plywood-fronted panels. The door was to the right of the cubicle, and I approached it, stealing a glance outside through the window. The skies were turning gray, and there wasn't a sign of anybody. Maybe someone had stepped out and would be back soon. I didn't have long.

Inside Derrick's office, I was pleasantly reassured by the mess. This was his office alright. Empty coffee cups and fast-food cartons sat here and there, giving off a faint reek I remembered well. I shuddered at the thought that I was in the room of the man who'd done everything he could to entrap and control me, the man who hung like a shadow over my life. But I shook off my fears and started looking.

Trevor thought the case file would be somewhere no one else could find it, so that ruled out the filing cabinets and desk drawers. There had to be somewhere else.

At the back of the office was a crude metal table covered in box files and dividers. My eyes scanned it quickly, then darted to the underside of the table. *A safe!*

Unlike everything else in the office, it looked fairly new and in good condition. It was electric, too, plugged into an extension cable that ran the length of the wall to Derrick's desk, where a thick, black laptop lay undisturbed. I went over to the table and kneeled to inspect the safe.

A faint blue glow emitted from the screen, illuminating a keypad. I stared at it for a little while, my imagination running wild as to what I'd find in the safe. Four dashes were printed on the small screen. So it was a four-digit passcode.

I looked around me at the office desperately. There was no chance I'd be able to figure it out, even if I knew where to look.

Could I take the safe? Derrick might be gone for a while. If no one noticed it was gone, maybe I could get it back to Max's, and we could figure out how to open it? I sighed and slumped to the ground. What a ridiculous idea. Even if there was some chance I could lift the thing, what would Max say once I brought it home? That I was a thief? A madwoman, more likely. I stared at the safe for a while, and then it came back to me.

That dirty apartment block. The one we'd first lived in when I ran away to the mainland with Derrick. It had a passcode, didn't it? To get in? What was it? I racked my brain, delving deep into memories that were as unwelcome to me as I was in this office.

I took a deep breath. If I typed the wrong combination, Derrick would know for sure. The safe was probably alarmed.

I bent down and put 1 - 5 - 0 - 3 into the keypad.

A second of silence went by.

Then I heard a click.

Predictable.

The safe door unlocked, sliding slightly ajar. I couldn't believe it. "Should have thought harder before you set the code, Derrick," I said, pulling open the door to the safe.

A lot of stuff was crammed inside on its shelves. Two stacks of hundred dollar bills drew my eye right away. There was something else, a small plastic bag wrapped around itself, concealing a dark color inside. Was it...marijuana?

"Looks like you've been helping yourself to the evidence, Derrick," I said, smirking. If this guy was a straight cop, I was a magician.

The file was in a brown cardboard divider. I reached in and pulled it out. It wobbled in my hand. I opened it up:

ACCIDENT REPORT: BOSTON POLICE FORENSICS DIVISION

Below, in a series of inked square boxes, were handwritten notes. Mainland police had done a lot of the work for the sheriff's office, no doubt because they weren't prepared for this kind of thing. I flipped through the file. There were at least ten pages of reports and evidence about the crash. At the back of the file, I felt hard, thick paper. I knew there were photographs in there, but I didn't want to look. This was what I came here to find. I knew that much for sure. And I knew I'd better be going now.

I stood up, closed the safe, and walked right out of Derrick's office…and bumped into Trevor just as he was on his way in.

He started and stumbled, reaching for his gun. I screamed, dropping the file. We stood there on opposite sides of the doorway, staring at each other.

"SOPHIE?" he yelled, incredulous. "What the hell are you doing here, sis?"

I stooped to pick up the file, then stood, head bowed.

Just my luck to get arrested by my own brother.

I couldn't bring myself to say anything. I was pretty sure everything in Trevor's brain was screaming at him to cuff me then and there.

But he didn't. He put his gun back in its holster.

"Sophie," he said, with a low tone of voice that made me tremble a little. "What's that in your hand?"

***

I don't think I'd ever seen my brother laugh as hard.

"You!" He wheezed, bending over double as he sat on one of the desks. "You cracked his safe? Oh man, I can't tell you how many hours I've spent wondering how to get into that thing, and you just…"

"It's not FUNNY, Trevor!" I said. "I broke the law coming here, but I had to."

That shut him up. "Yeah," he said, regaining control of himself. "I guess you did. But you broke the law to obtain a police report that Derrick didn't want anyone to see. A police report about one of the most serious incidents on this island in the last ten years. I don't know, Sophie. I'm not exactly gonna book you for it."

"Well, I appreciate that," I said. "But look, Trevor, what does it mean? I don't understand any of the stuff that's written."

"I'll need time to look at it," he said. "And..." he added wryly, "...time to swap out the security footage from those cameras." He pointed up, and I followed his finger to where a sinister black glass eye was swiveling, a witness to me breaking and entering.

"How'd you figure it out, though?" said Trevor. "That's what I don't get. The passcode."

"Long story," I said. "Let's just say Derrick doesn't have a very active imagination when it comes to security."

He nodded. "I won't pry."

"Can I...can I have it, Trevor?"

He looked at me. "No way. This is a police report. If you take it out of here with you, then I really will have to arrest you. This is better off with me, Sophie. Trust me. I'll find out what's in here."

"Trevor, I *need* that report for Max. He isn't going to be himself until he knows the truth."

"Max is gonna be just fine without reading this. Trust me, if what I think is in here is in here, it's going to be an unpleasant read."

I felt myself growing impatient. "Trevor, that's not fair. Max has a right to know more than anyone."

"As far as I'm concerned, you and Max should be focusing on the future right now," replied Trevor.

"What's that supposed to mean?"

"I mean that you two guys are together. Oh, come on, Sophie, don't try and hide it. I know, and I'm not exactly the world's greatest mind reader. Don't you have stuff to sort out between yourselves right now?"

"No. As a matter of fact, Trevor, we don't. Max and I are perfectly fine as we are."

Trevor laughed, but there was nothing humorous about it this time. "Yeah. I'll bet."

"What are you even getting at Trevor? Is there something I should know about Max?"

He looked down, embarrassed. I'd always been able to tell when Trevor was hiding something, ever since he was little.

"What is it?" I said.

He didn't reply.

"Trevor, you're scaring me. What is it?"

"There is something you need to know. But you need to hear it from Max, not me." There was shame in Trevor's voice like he'd broached a long-kept secret.

"What is it? What does he need to tell me?"

When Trevor looked up, it was with sorrowful eyes. "It's about Bee," he said.

Chapter 22

Max

"I can only tell you what I've found, Max. And it doesn't look good. Who'd you say this Locklow fellow was again?"

"Give me a second, Paul. Just let me think for a minute."

Paul Grigson was considerably less lethargic as he shared his findings with me over the phone, but I wasn't ready to hear what he had to say. I paced the corners of my living room with the printed files on my desk, looking out into the darkness. Mindy was sitting in a chair, reading one of her books. I kept giving her anxious glances, trying not to betray just how rattled I was. I steeled myself.

"He's my brother-in-law. He wouldn't do this kind of thing."

"Well, I think you need to have a serious talk with him, Max. The problem wasn't storage *or* manufacturing. It was materials. This fella, Winston. He's been buying inferior wood in large quantities, then aging and distressing it to give it the appearance of the product you're selling."

"Paul," I said. "You need to be sure about this. One hundred percent. What you're accusing Winston of here is fraudulent—illegal, even."

"Well, I can't prove criminal liability, Max. I'm just a business analyst. But I've got plenty of evidence. Phone conversations, emails, reports. All of it. Your server guys were very helpful. Winston's been buying inferior, unsustainable timber and sneaking it into the stock for Fircress Furniture products. I'd say your options are pretty clear at this point, wouldn't you?"

"Yeah. I would. Thank you, Paul."

"Sorry it had to be me, Max."

"That's alright. Send me the bill."

I put the phone down and looked at Mindy. She looked up from her book. I went over to her and kneeled down.

"Sweetie, daddy has to go to the guesthouse for a little bit. Mind if Mrs. Langley does bedtime tonight?"

Mindy shook her head.

On the way out, I saw Mrs. Langley. "Mrs. Langley, could you do me a favor? I need to go up to the guest house to see Winston. Can you put Mindy to bed for me?"

She looked at me. "Of course, Max. But, I need to get home pretty soon—"

"I understand," I said. "Once she's in bed and the lights are off, please feel free to leave and lock the door."

"But, Max," said Mrs. Langley. "Where's Sophie?"

I sighed. "I'm not sure, Mrs. Langley. We've both got a lot on our plate right now. Really appreciate you helping."

"It's no trouble," she said, but I could see the wariness in her eyes. She knew something wasn't right with me.

I put my coat on by the front door and a pair of boots. I wasn't sure what I expected to find up there. I suspected that when I saw Winston, I'd have a hard time restraining myself from kicking his ass. How could he do this to me?

Ever since Winnie and I founded the company, we wanted to ensure we used only the finest natural products. Sustainable timber was the first thing we sourced—it didn't come cheap, but the furniture was better. And even if it lasted longer, people kept buying it from us because they trusted it to last. Winston was about to sabotage that expectation of quality with his short-term profiteering.

I closed the door and locked it. I thought about Sophie guiltily as I paced up the hill. Where was she right now? And how was I going to work up the courage to tell her the truth...that, two years ago, her sister had kissed me while I was stone-drunk in a bar in town?

As I approached the guesthouse, I saw the curtains were closed. Was Winston even in there? I approached the door, but it was locked. "The cheek of this guy," I said to myself as I reached into my pocket for the spare key. Did he really think I didn't have one?

Inside it was dark. I passed by the first two rooms of the house, a modestly-sized kitchen and a small lounge with a sofa and a reading lamp. None of the lights were on. There was no way Winston was here. He'd up and vanished—probably the moment he'd got wind that I'd hired Paul Grigson to look over the accounts.

At the back of the guesthouse was a bedroom. The bed was unmade and had been slept in. Beside it was a wine glass and a paperback novel strewn over the bedside table. He'd knocked them over. Probably leaving in a hurry.

I pulled out my cell phone and dialed the number for my head of security at my company offices. It rang for a few seconds, then a voice answered quickly and politely.

"Mr. Fircress, how can I help you today?"

"Alan, is Winston there?"

"No, sir. Mr. Locklow has been out all day. Meeting with a developer, I believe. He declined an offer of transport to the meeting."

"That's just grand. Alan, I'd like you to restrict Winston Locklow's security pass to Level 1 and bar him from using the lift. He is not to enter the office until he's spoken to me personally."

"Sir? We're shutting out...your brother-in-law?"

"That's right, Alan. Let me know if there are any problems." I gave the ID verification and hung up. *This ought to show you, you greedy little asswipe.*

Adjacent to the bedroom was an office that looked out onto the front of my workshop. Inside was a laptop perched on the desk next to the office computer I'd had installed. Unsurprisingly, Winston hadn't been keen to log onto my personal server. My bet was that he was using a VPN to access the internet privately from the guesthouse. That way, there was no chance I would have known what he was up to, even if I'd wanted to check. I felt a simmering, sickly feeling of betrayal rising in my stomach.

I searched the drawers, anxious to see if he'd left behind anything in his desk about my company. The first draw contained nothing of interest—the same documents I had access to, hell, the same documents any of the executives at Fircress Furniture had. I opened the second drawer, rifling through its contents before my eyes landed on two sets of documents.

The first was baffling. It was a set of blueprints or architectural plans for something. It was clearly part of a bigger file, and I wouldn't know what it was until I'd seen the whole thing. But the second piece of paper was all too familiar. It had been seven years since I'd filled one in, but I knew what a federal application for planning permission looked like.

The two sites in question were familiar to me—Breaker's Point Creek and Westmoorlands. They were the two patches of land Winston had acquired on the east side of the island. My brother-in-law was planning to bulldoze the east side of the island. I looked at the plans. I didn't know what it was he wanted to build there. Frankly, I didn't care.

I was simmering with rage as I left the house. In the darkness, my phone screen lit up with an eerie blue color as I called him. It went straight to voicemail, but that didn't stop me.

"Winston, you're out. I'm still a majority shareholder in this company, and you know what that means for you. Until you come to talk to me about this mess you've created, you can forget anything to do with Fircress Furniture again. You've pissed off the wrong guy, *old man.*"

I hung up. He'd have no choice but to come to me now.

As I came back down to the house, I saw the Jeep parked in the driveway. I started to break into a light jog. She was back! Sophie was home.

I'd left the porch light on for her, but I was surprised to see the speed at which she jumped out of the car and marched up to the house. "Sophie!" I called out as I carried on jogging down the hill, off the track, and straight toward the house. She didn't hear me.

I sidestepped through a bed of ferns and flowers. Their petals were already cast off by the cooler weather we'd been having. "Sophie!" I called again, but she still stood at the door, fumbling with her key in the lock. I was jogging across the beds, trying to get to her.

As I rounded the side of the house, I stopped. Her eyeline was level with mine now. She shot me a look, sad and furious all at once.

It was then that I realized that she knew.

Chapter 23

Sophie

I wasn't interested in anything he had to say. I marched up the stairs to my room. Max followed me, calling my name. But it was like I was watching the whole world through a movie screen. We might have been underwater for all I knew.

In my room, I lifted my bag onto the bed, where it landed with a thump.

"Sophie," Max said once again.

"You can stop saying my name...like it changes anything," I replied. I pulled open my chest drawers, three at a time, and threw open the closet. Inside were the few sets of clothes and shoes I'd brought with me to Criker's Isle, plus a few things Max had picked up for me. I didn't have the time or inclination to sort through any of it, so I took the neatly folded piles and began to throw them into my suitcase.

"What are you doing?" said Max. "I messed up, Sophie, I know that, but let's just talk about this—"

I carried on folding and putting the piles of clothes into the bag. I had a thousand questions inside, most of which began with: *Why?* But I held them in. I didn't want to say anything. With every step I took, I felt myself grow a little colder, a little more used to ignoring him. The light he'd shone on my life had all but gone out.

Max reached over me, desperate. I wanted to push him away, but something stopped me, and I stood there, frozen, hands in the air, as he clumsily reached over my things. "Let's stop, let's just stop and talk about this for a moment," he said, gentle but a little manic.

"Talk about what, Max?" I heard myself say. It was like I was watching myself act.

He said nothing, just stood there. It made me unspeakably mad.

"Talk about *what?*" I repeated. It was like all the rage I'd buried down was coming up, erupting out of me. And Max was in the way of it.

"I can explain—" he began, moving around from the other side of the bed to be nearer to me. But I wanted him to stay away and made it known, squaring up to him, ridiculous as it must have seemed.

"How could you explain that? You could have explained it before you kissed me, Max. Before we started seeing each other. You can't explain it now. Now it's just a *lie*. A shitty, cruel lie."

"I meant to tell you, Sophie, I really did. But I didn't want you to be upset."

"Too bad! Too bad you didn't want me to be upset. I am upset, Max. I'm incredibly upset. Because of you. Because you didn't tell me. Because you lied."

"Goddamit, Sophie, it was just a kiss! A stupid kiss!" He tried to put his hands on me, but I brushed them off.

"I don't care! It doesn't matter what happened. It might not have, Max, it really might not have if you had just told me. You knew things between Belinda and me were bad. You knew, and yet you didn't say anything. I can't trust you anymore! I was ready to be yours, and you pushed me away, you, you—"

I didn't have the words to finish. I thumped him on the chest with both my hands as I said the words, and then, before I knew it, I'd flung myself into his arms.

And soon after, we were kissing, rough and passionate.

He pushed me over onto the bed, and I pulled him with me. I'd never held him so tightly as I did then, and my hands scrabbled at the buttons of his shirt. I'd only undone a few before I felt myself reach under it and hold him as hard as I could, etching scratch marks into his back. While I did, he kissed me, his lips and teeth tracing a course over my mouth, my ears, and my neck until they settled on my chest when he pulled at my jeans.

I pushed him onto his back. I didn't know what I wanted— though I knew I wanted him and knew it would be on my own damn terms. Nothing about this would be his—it was a selfish act to take, not to give.

I unzipped my jeans and pulled them off before I did the same to him. While I did, his hands tried to wrestle mine away, like he wanted me to be slower. But I was so sick of everything now, and I felt him, hard for me under his jeans, and knew that having him here, now, would be the way out.

I leaned down and kissed him, one of my hands roughly grabbing at his scalp while he took me in his hands and felt every inch of his body but now bucked and strained against him for control. We rutted like animals. I reached down, taking his cock in my hands and warming it, feeling it grow in my hands and feeling powerful, in control. While I jerked him off slowly, I bent over and kissed him, put the other hand on my breast, and made him gently squeeze, cupping them, making me feel wanted.

I couldn't escape it any longer. I mounted him, feeling that exceptional cock of his enter me, sighing in relief. I rested my hands on top of him and began to rock back and forwards. Max groaned, as did I. We didn't speak, didn't say a word to one another, as I took what I wanted, rocking my hips back and forth faster now, bending over him.

"Say you love me," I said. "Say you love me."

"I do," he said. "I do, Sophie."

"Say it."

"I love you. I-I love you, Sophie."

"I love you," I said, beginning to move up and down the shaft of his cock. I was riding him hard now, both my hands on his chest while I straightened my back. We fucked like that for a while until my legs burned, and I was brought to the brink of orgasm, watching him below me, the wonderful way his face looked as I fucked him, eyes wide, his mouth open with longing for me.

"That's it," I said. "Come for me, baby."

He looked at me, and one of my hands reached out and stretched over his face to rest on his cheek.

"That's it," I said again. "Come for me, Max, please, please, please."

He didn't disappoint me.

***

Fifteen minutes later, I was dressed. Max still lay in a daze on the bed. As I pulled on my pants, I saw him sit up and watch me.

"You're..." he said. Then I watched him as he saw the packed bag by the doorway of the room. "You're going?" he said.

I couldn't look at him. The shame of what we'd just done was too great. What was worse was that I enjoyed it so much.

"You...you betrayed me," I said quietly, trying not to cry and be brave for him. "You betrayed my trust, Max. I don't want to see you again. And I don't think I can work for you now. Not after this."

In the distance, a police siren blipped.

"That's Trevor," I said. I'd already called him and asked him to come and get me.

Max sat up and pulled on his jeans.

"Mindy's asleep. Are you going to say goodbye to her?" he said, a cold fire burning in his eyes.

He'll hate you forever for leaving his daughter like this, said the voice in my head.

I shook my head. "I can't."

I went down the stairs and opened the front door, my bag in hand. Trevor had turned off his horn, but the lights on the top of the squad car were still flashing, red, blue, red, blue.

I closed the door behind me. The lights ran over it like they were illuminating a crime scene.

Chapter 24

Max

It rained so heavily the night after Sophie left that I couldn't sleep. And by the time it had stopped, and I was able to stand out on the porch, watching the lights of Fairtown in the dark, wondering where she was, it was cold. Freezing, actually.

In the morning, a thick blanket of frost had covered the grass outside. It was cold in the house too, and I made sure to turn the burner up before Mindy woke. I couldn't sleep, of course, not without knowing where she was. And this time, the pain in my chest was searing, burning me to the point where I could hardly think straight. It was almost as though something was catching up to me from the past.

Sunday came and went, rainy and cold. Mindy didn't feel like going outside. A few times, we had the awful conversation that would become our habit over the next few days.

"Where's Sophie?" Mindy said, curious.

"Sophie's gone on holiday, sweetheart. She needs...she needs a rest." Lying to my own daughter wasn't one of my proudest moments, but how could I have told her the truth? She'd hate me if I told her I'd driven Sophie away, that it was my fault.

"When's she coming back?"

"I'm not sure, pumpkin."

Mindy was quiet for a little while. Then she spoke again.

"I miss Sophie," Mindy said.

"Me too," I replied.

I did my best with her, and I did, but by the end of the day, she was quiet and withdrawn. She was still happy to talk, but I could tell she longed for Sophie's calming, peaceful presence as much as I did.

The next day, I drove Mindy to school. I made sure she had all her things and the lunch I'd hastily made in the morning before sending her to the school gates. I was about to turn the car around and head back through town to Fairview, but the pain gripped me again before I could turn on the engine. It was like a knife running through me.

Beyond the school, out past the few cottages and fisherman's houses that sat around it, I could see the hills, bleak and forlorn, and wondered about the road which lay up there.

There was only one place I felt I could go.

So I drove west, out of town, up the road towards the village where Sophie's parents lived. But this time, I turned right at the crossroads, taking the Jeep down a narrow lane towards the church at the bottom. It was abandoned on a Monday. There was nobody there, and the island's congregation had dwindled to the point where even the dirt track by the old stone building was rough and filled with potholes. Muddy water splashed the wheel guards of the jeep as I pulled up and got out.

Things were much the same as they were the last time I was

there. A poplar tree sat in the corner of the graveyard. I walked among the rows of battered and weathered stones for a while before making my way to the end of the yard, where a single white stone stood amongst all the gray ones. On it was a date that marked a thirty-two-year-long life. Below it, there was a simple inscription:

WINIFRED AMY LOCKLOW

Sister to Winston

Wife to Max

Mother to Mindy

I knelt by the grave. I pulled my hand inside the sleeve of my windbreaker and wiped away a few leaves that had settled inside its border. I hadn't brought flowers. She never liked flowers.

"Me again, captain," I said. That was what I called her.

Of course, there was no answer, no greeting. There never was, but I still spoke all the same.

"I need your help," I said. "Again. Bet that doesn't surprise you. See, I've made a mistake."

I heard the rustling of the wind in the trees and felt a few light spots of rain fall on my face. I looked up into the gray mizzen and mist of the sky.

"I met someone. You always said—" I winced on my own words and then continued. "You always said that if something happened to you, I ought to get remarried. I think we were joking around at the time. Didn't know I'd ever have to think about that."

There was another rustle, not from the leaves of the trees but from the overgrown hedge which sat to my left at one end of the churchyard.

I looked up to where a swallow dipped through the rainy, gray air above the church. Then, out of the corner of my eye, I saw it. There was a fox hidden behind the hedge. My eyes caught a glimpse of its red fur as it darted out of sight again.

"I really like her. I-I love her. But I let her down, made a mistake, and didn't tell her. The thing is, Win, I need her. I need her back, but, I can't. I can't just..."

If I listened, I could hear tiny noises, rustlings of dry grass here and there. The silence in the graveyard was overwhelming.

"And Winston, too. He's not...he's not who we thought he was, Win. I just wanted to come by because I don't know what to do, Win. I'm scared. I've been so scared, scared for the last three years. Afraid for Mindy, afraid to live. And Sophie makes me feel something...something I haven't felt in a long time. She makes me brave."

All kinds of tiny clicks in the grass, no doubt the noises of beetles and bugs, joined the occasional howl of the wind.

"I came here to tell you I've met someone. And I'm not going to let anything get in the way of us. Not your brother or his misguided intentions. But I've got to sort it all out first, Win."

I stood up.

"I've got to sort it out."

I began to walk to the gate of the churchyard. There was something so still about that place that it amplified the noise of the world around it. Behind me, I heard a click, like someone had stepped on a twig. I turned around.

The fox had come through the hedge. I studied its wise face for a moment and saw the dark glint of its wide, brown eyes.

The fox looked at me for a moment, then disappeared into the undergrowth.

***

From the window of the car, I watched Mindy leave the school. Her bag swung over her shoulder, and she was carrying her sketchbook. It was folded open so that a dazzling display of color, the burnished oranges and bright reds of the sunset, swayed along behind Mindy's arm as she walked. I stepped out of the car. She looked up. Then looked down when she saw me.

"Hey, Min," I said as she got into the car. "How was school?"

She said nothing but looked down at the sketchbook in her lap.

"Sophie usually comes to get me from school," she said slowly.

I sighed heavily and put the keys in the ignition.

"When we get back to the house, we're gonna pack our bags."

"Why?" said Mindy curiously.

"We're taking a little trip," I said. I'd decided to take us to the mainland for a while. It would be good for Mindy to see the city and have a change. Things were going to be weird for her without Sophie, and I needed to deal with the problems in front of me. I had business to take care of now that Winston was on indefinite leave from Fircress Furniture. And another idea was already brewing in my mind.

I was going to get Sophie back, no matter what.

A few hours later, night had fallen by the time we arrived at the airfield. Mindy was tired and cranky. I gathered her things out of the back of the Jeep. I'd taken the long way round the coastal road. I couldn't bring myself to drive up the hill. I felt brokenhearted and beaten down as I put Mindy's two little suitcases on the ground and produced mine, a somewhat larger one. Sophie had only been with us for nearly three months now, but we felt her absence as though she'd been a part of our lives for much longer.

Craig Gardner came out of his cabin to meet us. He'd known nothing of our relationship and warmly shook my hand, even if there was a hint of embarrassment on his face.

"How are you doing, Max? I've got her all fueled up. Jake will fly you tonight, though. I'm spending some time at home with my family."

"Not to worry, Craig," I said. "I'm grateful you could fit us in. It's short notice, I know. Something came up with the company."

He nodded, then looked at the plane behind us for a while. Jake was standing beside it, in his bomber jacket, performing the pre-flight checks.

"I, uh...I'm sorry it didn't work out with you folks, Max. I know Sophie got on well with your daughter."

"How is she, Craig?" I asked.

He looked at me suspiciously. *With good reason*, I thought.

"It's none of my business, of course," I said. "I'm just...well, I'm fond of her, is all. Want to make sure she's somewhere safe."

"She's at home with us at the moment, actually. Huge help around the house. She's...well, she's my daughter and all, but Sophie...well, she's a godsend."

I nodded, smiling as a shiver of emotion ran through me. "She certainly is."

Craig looked at his shoes. "Not much work for a childminder

round here, though. She thinks she might teach at the school for a while. Not sure, though."

"Craig," I said. "Could you...could you tell Sophie something for me? I understand if it's too much, or—"

"I'll tell her, Max," he said, and I could see there was a hint of sadness in his voice. "Sophie's done a lot for us all, mind. The least we could do is think about what she wants. About what's best for her. Understand?"

I nodded. The look in his eye was protective, fierce, even. I was glad people were looking out for her like that. "I just want you to tell her..." I said guiltily, "...that she's welcome back whenever she's ready. *If* she's ready."

Craig nodded and smiled, a wistful smile that told me he understood what was going on between us. "Well, I guess it's time you folks were heading off," he said briskly and began to walk back to the cabin.

I watched him go before picking up Mindy's bags and making my way toward the plane. As I did, I heard my phone ring and laughed as Jake stepped forward to help me with the bags.

"Easy there, Mister Fircress," said Jake. "I'll take care of those. You answer your phone."

"Thanks, Jake," I said, pulling it out of my pocket.

"Max?" the voice on the other end of the line was crackly and static out here in the woods. "This is Greg Douglass." Greg was my lawyer.

"Hey Greg," I said. "I've got to catch a flight in ten, but I just wanted to give you an update. I've got two very important things to discuss with you."

Chapter 25

Sophie

I took a look into the shimmering pool. It was a frosty day on Criker's Isle, the cold mists that had seeped in overnight condensed into beads of dew on the grass beside me as I stood at Folly Falls.

The Falls were one of the island's most famous attractions. They began a little way up the hill, where precipitation from Mount Criker had dug a fast-flowing torrent of water into the earth, which came crashing over a basalt cliff into the local river. One arm of the river led straight out to the sea, but the other, still raging and coursing down the slopes of the mountain, cascaded over rocks and fell in a glorious spray towards the gleaming pool in front of me.

When we were kids, the Falls had been a rite of passage for any teenager brought up on the island, and taking a dip there in winter was a much-loved test of endurance and strength. The last time I'd jumped into the pool was almost fifteen years ago. Bonus points, I fondly recalled, were awarded to the bravest swimmers, who would dip their heads under the waterfall.

I was back home with my parents. It was an unusual feeling to be sleeping in the bedroom I'd grown up in. Trevor and I were reunited under the same roof. Not that I saw much of him. He was too busy managing things on the Isle during Derrick's absence and spent the rest of his time locked away, studying the report I'd stolen from the sheriff's office.

In the meantime, I helped fix up the house a little with my dad or joined my mom on her long rambles into the wilderness. I'd already joined her on one or two excursions up to where Winston Locklow's name loomed out on signs nailed into the bark of ancient trees or rested on the occasional gates that were still maintained during the off-season.

This place was changing; it wasn't the place I'd left all those years ago, despite how much of my past had confronted me since I returned. Seeing those signs made me think of Max and Mindy. Each day I'd spent away from that house brought a new ache to my insides. I wondered where Mindy was and who was looking after her. Thinking about Max flooded my head with memories of him, his smile, his strong shoulders, his shabby, rugged outdoor clothes.

My dad had told me the night Max and Mindy had left for the mainland. Or, more accurately, I'd wrung the information reluctantly out of him. It had been a week since they'd left, a week of loneliness and separation from the people I cared the most about, a week of waking up to look at the missed calls and texts from Max. Each day I promised myself I'd write back to him, and each day I never managed it. I knew I'd speak to him when the time was right, but for now, I retraced my steps on the island like a ghost. I visited teenage haunts, like the Falls, and thought about the past, what had been lost, and what could be saved.

I made up my mind to take the jump, and after looking around to make sure no one would be watching, I removed the thick woolen jumper I'd borrowed from my mom and folded it gently on the plastic bag I'd brought so that the clothes wouldn't get wet. I stood on my towel as I removed my shoes and socks. Then, I unbuttoned my jeans. The air was bracing, and for a moment, I stood shivering on the precipice, looking down into the dark water below.

It was only now I'd begun to realize how much my life had been ruled by fear, the fear of Derrick, the fear of what others thought. I was determined not to be ruled by fear any longer, and so after a moment of hesitation, I held my nose, closed my eyes, and stepped off the ledge.

As I hit the water, the impact was followed by soundless darkness that rushed around my eyes and left me lost to oblivion before water flooded into my nose and mouth.

I quickly kicked my legs out of instinct rather than of any desire to reach the surface. My head broke the water, and suddenly I was looking up, above the trees which surrounded the pool, the treetops and the birds flying above, and the dull, cold white light of the winter sun. I took an enormous gasp and steadied myself, beginning to move my arms and paddle, lest they freeze.

Freedom.

I stayed there for maybe a minute or more, controlling my breathing, letting the icy water rejuvenate and purge me of everything I'd been holding onto. It was practically a spiritual experience, secret, dangerous, something that was mine and mine alone. When I finally hauled myself out of the water and sat, shivering in my underwear on the stone ledge on the other side of the pool, I was laughing, my body flooding with dopamine, alive and alert to anything which might come.

I leaped up the boulders which bridged the water's edge from the grassy knoll it was situated upon and walked around. I was doubled over with cold, but inside me, there was nothing but a quiet sense of peace and joy. For a moment, I'd forgotten about everything, but slowly, as the world came back into focus and I frantically began to rub myself dry with the towel I'd brought, only one thought came to my mind.

I want him.

I stopped for a while, frightened of what else the voice inside of me would say. Max had betrayed me, lied to me, and it still hurt. And yet, he'd given me so much more. Was it possible I'd forgive him? Did I have it in me? I didn't know.

Just then, out of the corner of my eye, I saw someone walking through the woods a hundred yards or so below the treeline. I grabbed my jumper and jeans and pulled them on quickly, as much out of a desire to protect myself from the freezing cold as to protect my modesty. When I looked up again, I saw the figure standing in a familiar puffed windbreaker, scraping her hair back from behind her ears.

"That sounded like some jump," she said. "I heard it from the trail below."

I looked at her and studied her face, a little rounder than mine, more wind-chafed by years of hard living on the island. Some part of me wanted to shout at her, to ask her what she was doing here. But immediately, I thought of the cool water which lay below, glanced back, and saw its shimmering, calm ripples beat back by the foaming spray of the Falls. It was like I'd never disturbed its surface at all.

"What are you doing up here?" I said.

"Ain't it obvious?" Belinda replied, squinting a little as she looked at me in the sunlight. "Mom said you'd be up here."

"You came by the house?"

Belinda nodded, looking around in that way she had. I knew she had plenty to say, but for some reason, she wasn't saying it. I picked up my towel and rubbed my hair.

"You wanted to talk to me, didn't you?"

"I guess I did." Belinda's voice sounded different from when I'd seen her for dinner and when she appeared in Max's garden a month ago. She was different, altogether quieter, softer.

"Well, no time like the present, Bee," I said, raising an eyebrow.

Belinda looked at me. Gradually her eyes widened, and she walked up towards me through the grass, stopping at the edge of the pool. We were almost on opposite sides.

"I guess I wanted to get a few things straight."

I looked at her. My big sister. Belinda had always been the taller of us, the stronger. Now, in the cold light by the pool, she looked weak, even a little beaten down. I felt myself growing more irritated, wanting to leave, but then the voice which had spoken to me by the water's edge spoke again.

It said: *if you don't speak first, this won't end.*

"I'm sorry," I said. I heard the words echo a little bit around the glade before they were lost to the roaring of the Falls.

Belinda looked at me quizzically. She stared for a little while, then said, "Why?"

"I didn't know, Bee. I didn't know what had happened between you and Max. I didn't know you—I mean, I didn't know there was something there. Something that would make it hard for you to see me in his house, looking after his kid."

Belinda eyed me warily, searching for any sign of deception. Seeing none, she spoke.

"It was around ten, eleven, maybe. We were in The Red Rod.

I couldn't sleep in my apartment. I went for a walk and found him there. He's...he's a handsome guy, Sophie. You know that."

I nodded. So she knew—or had guessed—about me and Max. "I'm sorry I didn't tell you. I wish I had, so you would have told me what happened."

"He's never—I mean, he never felt the same way about me, as I..." said Belinda. She hesitated to finish the sentence. I understood. Belinda might have wanted Max, but for him, it was just an accident. A mistake. Like he'd said.

So he was telling the truth.

"Nothing like that ever happened again, Sophie. I promise. He's a good guy. And dad says that he wants you back—that he misses you."

There was hurt on her face now like she was fighting something inside her, that cruel part of her that had done so much to belittle and hurt me in our lives.

"The truth is, Sophie, I'd give anything to be you. To have...to have someone like that in your life. It made me jealous. It made me unkind. I haven't been the best sister for many years. I don't think I ever was, and I'm sorry."

I nodded. "I haven't exactly been the nicest to you."

She waved a hand as if to stop me from apologizing. I could see that Belinda had begun to cry.

I took three steps toward her, then I stopped. "Can we try..." I said slowly, calmly, still fed inner peace by the pool below, "...to be at peace? I don't want you to like me, and I don't need you to forgive me. But can we try that? For mom and dad? For Mindy and Max? For Trevor, for all the people we care about?"

Belinda looked away, and I heard her sobbing pitifully. Then I saw her make one slow nod.

"We can try," she said as she sniffled. "Somehow." She looked up at me, smiling through the tears.

"Good."

"What will you do, Sophie? Will you go back to him?"

I looked past her, through the trees. There was a gap in the hills there, on the western edge of the mountainside, where you could see down, across the flats, towards the sea. It was like an opening, a gateway to something else.

"I know one thing. I'm leaving."

"You're leaving?" Belinda looked shocked. "Why? Have you told Mom and Dad?"

"Not yet. But I need to get out, Bee. It's not right for me to be here right now."

Belinda looked like she wanted to argue, to criticize, but suppressed it.

"If you're leaving..." she said, "...probably better to do it sooner rather than later."

"Why's that?" I said.

"Dad showed me the flight roster when I came by the house this morning. Derrick came back last night. Him and that Locklow guy. Are they friends?"

Chapter 26

Max

Life has a funny way of catching you up, doesn't it? You can't run from anything. But try to hide from a problem, and it finds you. And sometimes, all it takes to make you see that are the words of a child.

I'd spent a week on the mainland, shuttling back from my offices to my hotel while we tried to work out what had been happening. It was clear by now that Winston, while an expert at covering his tracks, had been stealing from the company. By passing off inferior models of our furniture as the real thing, he'd managed to accrue enough profits to keep our shareholders happy and to keep me from thinking anything was amiss. In room after room, on the floors of my company's HQ, I stood or sat and tried to justify my brother-in-law's deception to worried executives, accountants, and managers. We were still putting together a comprehensive picture of his misdeeds, but in the meantime, I'd notified Trevor. If Winston arrived on the mainland, he could at least inform me.

Meanwhile, Winston hadn't spoken a word to me. He'd sure spoken to his lawyers, though. Accusations of slander and libel were already falling at my door. It was going to be a gargantuan effort to assuage the fear of shareholders. And when the news broke, and the media got involved...well, that was going to present its own problems. I couldn't believe he'd stab me in the back like this. But I was still holding on, foolishly, to the idea that he could be saved. I felt sure my brother-in-law would come through once we'd talked things out.

In the middle of all this, the mess and the infighting and backstabbing of grown-up life, Mindy had shrunk out of view. I'd hired a nanny in the city, a nice enough girl who could watch her in our hotel suite at the Regal while I went back and forth from the office. In the evenings, she mostly stayed in, drawing or watching cartoons. Pictures of her and Sophie were already littering the lounge of our suite, and I noticed them when I came in during the evening.

"How is she?" I said.

The nanny stood up from where she'd been reading a book on the couch. I thought she was a nice enough girl but a little young for the job.

"I've seen her better," she said meekly. "Doesn't talk too much, does she?"

I sighed and went into Mindy's room. It was the perfect size for a child, but she hadn't touched anything in there. Not even the fruit the nanny had left on her nightstand had been eaten. Mindy was looking at some cartoons.

"You okay, sweetie?" I said.

"I want Sophie," she replied.

I sighed. "I know, honey. I want Sophie too."

She looked at me. "When are we going back? Sophie's going to be worried about us."

I looked at her miserably. "I know, baby. When we get back to Criker's Isle, we'll see Sophie."

Mindy looked away apathetically. It tore me up to see her like this. I cursed myself for ever letting Sophie leave, for not telling her the truth, for everything.

"Daddy, why are we here?" Mindy asked.

I kneeled by her side and brushed her curly hair. "I tried to tell you this yesterday, sweetheart. Daddy's got something important to talk about with the people at the company. Uncle Winston...well, Uncle Winston and Daddy are arguing about something."

"Is it 'cause Winston hurt Mommy?"

I froze.

"Mommy's gone, sweetheart. Don't you know that?" I was paranoid and anxious, but as I reached out to comfort her, Mindy swatted my arms away.

"I *know* that," she said. "But when Mommy wasn't dead, Uncle Winston *hurt* her."

The words stung me. It was the first time Mindy had ever admitted Winnie was gone, that she wasn't coming back. I peered at her, the rose-tinted veil I'd been wearing slipping away before me, my heart beginning to race.

"Mindy."

She didn't look at me.

"Mindy, this is really important, sweetheart. I don't understand you, and I need you to tell me some things."

She looked straight at me for the first time in a long time. Without even glancing away, she picked up the remote and turned off the TV. It was quiet in the hotel room, deathly quiet.

"*WHAT?*" she shouted, after a little while. Mindy never yelled, not now, not since Sophie had been with her. I was shocked.

"Mindy," I said quietly. "What did you mean when you said that Winston hurt Mommy?"

"Mommy said Winston was being bad," said Mindy. "They fought. *Bad.*"

"Do you know why Mommy and Winston were fighting?" I said, desperate now, feeling my heart pound like it was about to burst out through the wound on my chest.

"Mommy said Winston wanted to cut down trees," said Mindy, and suddenly, the scales fell from my eyes.

***

"Cessna 3306, you are cleared for landing, repeat, cleared for landing at Criker."

"Thanks, Craig. I've got Mr. Fircress and his daughter with me."

I looked out of the window as we dropped towards the island. I'd got us on the first flight back the minute the pieces all came together.

Winnie, Winston. That night on the road up to the airstrip. The accident. Derrick and Trevor's suspicions. Somehow it all seemed related. Had Winnie known about Winston's plans to develop the eastern side of the island? Had the two argued about it while I was away, in front of Mindy? I wasn't sure, but I was going to find out.

We touched down on the airstrip. I'd asked Mrs. Langley to be on standby in case I needed someone to watch Mindy. After the wheels of the propellor had stopped spinning, Jake unfastened his seatbelt and popped our doors. I got out, then reached into the back of the plane and lifted out Mindy, who had just been woken up by the landing.

At the edge of the field surrounding the airstrip, I could already see a police car. I watched by the gate for any sign of Derrick, but I breathed a sigh of relief when Trevor appeared from the darkness. As he approached, his face was grim.

"We need to talk," he said. In his file was a plastic wallet.

***

"This was the bit that I noticed," said Trevor.

We were sat in my living room. Mrs. Langley was putting Mindy to bed upstairs. Trevor had driven me straight over here, updating me on the situation. Derrick and Winston had come back that morning on a private, unregistered flight. Trevor hadn't known about it until Derrick marched into the office. He'd gotten out fast and gone up to the house to see if Winston was here, but he was staying somewhere else in town, probably at one of the B&Bs that were still trading this time of year.

In front of me, on my coffee table, was the police report for the accident which had injured me and killed Winnie. I tried to keep my eyes off the pictures, which were a horrible collage of twisted shrapnel and spilled gasoline. Instead, I looked at the document Trevor was showing me.

"D.A.I.A.R?" I said, bemused by the initials at the top of the report.

"Department of Automotive Incidents Analysis Report," said Trevor. "Clunky, I know, but basically, their main job is the forensic investigation of car crashes. They're the people who look at chassis damage, glass impact, and trauma on the body. And, in this case, tires."

"Tires?" I said. "What does it say?"

"A lot," said Trevor. "Believe me. I had to call up quite a few buddies from the academy while I was reading this. But here's the long and short of it."

"The official narrative..." he began, "...was that you lost control of the car. It aquaplaned, due to the rain, and that's why it went off the cliff. However, this report was never forwarded to the Coroner's Office or any of the officers who were on the scene by Derrick, who, as the lead investigator, had control over the reports."

"And what does this report say that Derrick buried?" I said, running my hands over the thin paper, staring at the words beneath me.

"It says that you blew a tire. Two tires, actually. And the damage is consistent with some kind of puncture wound delivered from below. These are smart guys, Max. They can tell from the condition of the rubber what's been done, and how much pressure the tires have been under after the crash. You suffered a blowout on the road. Do you remember anything like that?"

"No," I said. "At least, not that I remember. What I remember is..."

"Go on," said Trevor. "What is it?"

"I heard a bang. There was a jolt," I said. "Like I'd run over something."

Trevor's eyes widened. "I remember that from your statement. They thought you'd hit something or swerved. It's pretty common for people to remember the moment they lose control of a car pretty badly. But, Max, think hard now. What was the bang like?

Low-pitched, or high?"

I tried to think about it, blocking out the awful memories, Winnie's screams, the darkness. A noise like a gunshot came to my mind.

"High-pitched," I said. "I think. If it was the tires, someone must have jabbed something into them. Something sharp."

"Like a stinger?"

"A what now?"

"A stinger. Tire spikes."

"You think someone spiked my car?"

"Why not? They're easy to deploy and remove if you have the right set. They've been illegal for a while now. But certain people know how to get a hold of them. That could have been how you lost control of the car."

I was overwhelmed. I put my hands on my head.

"I'm sorry, Max, but I don't think what happened to Winnie was an accident. Do you know of anyone who could have hurt her?"

I looked up and caught a glimpse of my reflection in one of the enormous wall-to-ceiling windows in my living room. I looked practically ghoulish, furious, with eyes blazing. "Winston," I said. "Mindy was right, after all."

Then, I heard the doorbell. Trevor and I looked at each other.

"Expecting any visitors, Max?" said Trevor slowly. We both knew it wasn't going to look good if someone caught him here with a stolen set of police reports on my coffee table.

"No," I said. "I'll go to the door."

I went through the hallway, hearing the doorbell ring again.

Whoever it was, they were pretty insistent. "Is everything okay?" Mrs. Langley asked from upstairs.

"Everything's fine," I said tersely. "Just focus on Mindy."

When I opened the door, I saw Belinda standing there. She was soaking wet, and her shoes were slicked with mud. Her hair was wild and loose, flung about her shoulders by the wind. She was out of breath.

"Belinda?" I said incredulously. "Did you just...*run* up here?"

"I did," she said. "Is Trevor here? There's something you both need to know."

Chapter 27

Sophie

After the last plane landed for the night, the last ferry arrived. It was an old tradition on Criker's Isle, meaning anyone who missed the plane can get the ferry. It's not an easy ride. The crossing takes a few hours, and on the other side, the passengers are inevitably stranded until dawn.

Still, better than nothing.

I'd said an unexpected goodbye to my parents that evening and left with the few things I had. The walk down to town had been long and lonely in the setting sun. I'd stopped for something to eat at a café and moved on, walking through the sad old desolate town, my thoughts turning to its shabby storefronts and battered wooden boards.

Someone, someday, will help you, Fairtown. One day, you'll be worthy of the name.

As I watched the ferry come in, I turned and looked to my right, over the tops of the houses and up the hill, where there was a tiny speck of light, barely visible. That was Fairview, up there. I suddenly felt a twinge inside of me. Yesterday morning at the pool, where Belinda and I talked, I felt peace. But now I could only think about life without Max. I felt lost without him, like he was the thread that held me to this island. He'd pulled me back onto its shores, and now that I had lost him, I knew there was no way I'd be able to stay.

I looked across the sea into the night, where another light shone in the distance. It was the ferry coming into the harbor. I guess it would only be another ten minutes or so. That was where my new future lay. I could put this all behind me and start again. Perhaps.

It was quiet on the dock, except for the waves which lapped up against the jetty. In the darkness, I listened for anything that might guide me away from my present course.

I could swear that in the distance, I could hear Max calling my name. *Sophie.*

I turned my head and listened closer.

No. I could hear him calling my name.

"Sophie!" the voice cried, faint in the distance.

"Max?" I said to the wind. Then I called again, louder this time. "Max!"

I turned around and looked at the jetty behind me.

There he was!

I could see him striding through the darkness. I could have picked out his broad shoulders anywhere. He was dressed up for the cold, wearing a sheepskin jacket and pair of ski trousers. Was that...Trevor...next to him?

"Sophie!" they called and began to jog along the jetty towards me. They were rounding the corner onto the pier now.

"Max!" I yelled as he jogged under the streetlamps, phasing in and out of the darkness which surrounded us. "What are you doing?"

He stopped, maybe fifty yards from me.

"Sophie, don't go," he said.

Trevor was catching up to him. "We need you!" he said.

I looked at them both, the two men in the world besides my dad, who meant more to me than anything else. I could see their breath condensing in the cold before them. "How did you know where I'd be?" I said and took a step back. I didn't want them to stop me from boarding the ferry. I could hear its motor now as it came into the harbor.

"Sophie, I know I've hurt you, and I know you want to go. But please, don't do this," said Max. The desperation in his voice was unlike anything I had ever heard. He stood there as Trevor sidestepped him and came towards me.

"I'm not going to try to stop you from leaving," he said, watching my gaze as it flitted between them and the ferry. Its lamps were shining behind me now, and I could feel them illuminating the strange scene before us as we stood in a standoff on the jetty.

"Sophie, I know how to stop him. I know how to stop Derrick."

"Sophie, Derrick killed Winnie," Max said. "He killed my wife. And we're going to bring him in. Trevor has a plan. All we need is your help."

"Like hell I'm going near that psycho," I said. "And like hell I'm staying here to help you with whatever it is you've got planned. I wanted to help, Max. I wanted to be a part of your life. I wanted to be a part of Mindy's life. But you lied."

"That's right," said Max. "Everything you said is true. And it was wrong of me. And I'd do anything to make it up to you. But if you don't want to do this for me, Sophie, you don't have to. Do it for this place. For the island. For Trevor, and for your family, and everyone on this island and for..." his voice faltered, cracking in the chill winter air. "Do it for Winnie," he said. "She didn't do anything wrong, Sophie. She didn't hurt anyone."

I looked at them both, and they looked back. The ferry's horn sounded behind me, deafeningly loud. I clapped my hands over my ears, and suddenly, a memory flashed through my mind.

***

"You say goodbye?" said Derrick as he stood at the dock. I'd come alone, like he told me, bringing a bag of my favorite clothes, some CDs, and a few things as keepsakes.

"No," I said. *"But, Derrick, is this right? Do we need to do this? Why don't we go to my mom and explain things? I don't think..."* I trailed off, nervous to tell him how I really felt about all this.

Derrick took a step towards me. He was handsome. His sharp cheekbones stood out in the streetlamps and lights of the dock. *"Sophie,"* he said, sighing and shaking his head while he smiled. *"Oh, Sophie. Is that what you want? To go back home?"*

I looked down at my scuffed trainers and glanced around. Behind us, Fairtown was glimmering. The Christmas lights were on, and if you looked into the distance, you could see the crosswalk at the intersection of Main and West. Families were walking through, dressed in their winter coats. *"I don't know,"* I said. *"I'm just not sure."*

Derrick walked up to me and put his hands on my shoulders. His dark eyes shone under the lamps, giving him an otherworldly look. He reached up and scratched his short, bristly hair as he kept one arm around me.

"They..." he said, "...do not understand you. They don't know what you want. But I do, Sophie? Don't I?"

I nodded.

"Now, you and me, we're gonna get on that ferry. And once we land on the other side, that's it. I've got it all figured out, Sophie. We'll use those savings you got from your parents, get an apartment. I'll get a job. You can stay at home, do your drawings. We'll be family. We'll even get married." As I looked up at his eyes, practically gleaming with greedy desire for our new life, I sighed and shrugged my shoulders. "And your mom and your bitch sister, well, they'll just have to get used to it. We're going to have things **our** way, aren't we? And we can leave this dump behind and forget about it."

We got on the ferry. And some of what Derrick said came true. Most of it didn't, though. Most importantly, the last thing he said stuck with me. **Our way.** Because even when I got on the ferry, I knew it wouldn't be 'our way.' It would be his way every time. I'd hardly get a say. And somewhere inside me, the woman I'd one day become yelled at me not to go, not to leave it all behind, and I did anyway, and even then, as we sailed away into the night, the regrets and pains of years to come reached back at me from the future.

***

There was a long silence after the ferry's horn sounded. Max and Trevor had been just as startled by it as I was. Gradually, I opened my eyes and let my hands fall from around my ears. I looked at them, but my mind was made up already.

Firstly, I looked at Max. "When this is over..." I said.

"When this is over..." he said quietly, "...we can talk. Until then, all I want is to put things right. With you."

Trevor nodded. He looked at me. "Will you stay?" he asked.

I could see my breath in front of me, watched as the clouds coming from my heaving lungs gradually died down, and panic left my body. In its place, I felt a cold, hard feeling in my stomach, like stone, cold and lonely as the mountain which rose up, far above us in the darkness.

"What's the plan?" I said.

Chapter 28

Max

About half a mile out of town, up a track that ran parallel to the gorge by the airstrip, was a tiny hamlet. It had three or four houses. Two of them were abandoned, too derelict and rotten for other people to live in. I don't know who lived in the third house. But I knew who lived in the fourth, the one at the end of the cul-de-sac.

As Trevor and I sat in his squad car, quietly watching the house, we saw Sophie appearing out of the darkness from behind one of the houses.

She was alone, for all intents and purposes. I watched her standing in front of the house, squat, square, on two stories, with a porch and a pair of arched windows at the top that let scant daylight into the attic rooms.

There was an ugly feeling in me as I watched her walk up to that door. Sophie climbed the steps until she stood on the porch under a roof filled with crumbling shingles. I looked through the window on the right, through which I could see a grimy old kitchen with Formica worktops and a dining table, by the window. A ragged, dirty dishcloth was hung through one of the cupboard handles, which lay half-open. In it, I could see cans of food and bottles.

To the left, I could see the TV, its blue static light glowing in the room like a single blinking eye watching me. There was a couch up against the window and, by the fireplace, a chair. Derrick was sat in it, with something perched on his lap, dressed in nothing but a vest and a pair of pants, his eyes dully preoccupied with the war film playing on the TV. My eyes peered above his head, where I could see his shotgun, shining, deadly, over the fire. The mantlepiece was covered with chip wrappers and plastic drink cups, and, at one end, I could see his badge and gun, which he'd left up there. Derrick couldn't have looked less like he was expecting visitors.

Sophie stood there for a moment, and we braced ourselves before she rang the doorbell.

After a while, Derrick opened the door. Trevor leaned back in the seat of his car, motioning me to follow. We were invisible on that side of the street, but I craned my neck to see Derrick in the doorway.

He'd pulled on a shirt, though he hadn't bothered to button it up, and his feet were in a pair of boots, but he hadn't bothered to put any socks on, either. He opened the door and stood there. Trevor flicked a switch on his receiver, and we started to listen as the scene unfolded just fifty yards away.

"*Sophie?*" I heard him say.

I looked at him, trying for all the world to keep myself from stopping this now. I felt sure Sophie would run, but instead, she adjusted her feet and leaned on the doorframe. "Hi, Derrick," I heard her say.

He looked at her suspiciously, and then I saw him look out

beyond the door. He thrust it wide open and looked around at the porch, then directly at us. Trevor and I both took a deep breath of panic at the same time, but his eyes scanned the car lifelessly. He had no idea we were watching him.

"You with someone?" Derrick said quietly, dangerously.

"As a matter of fact, I'm not," Sophie replied. Her voice sounded light and almost childish through the microphone. "I guess you heard what happened with Max. I'm not working at Fairview anymore."

"Uh huh?" he said, and I saw him scratch the ragged strip of stubble around his chin. "Come by for a social call, then, is it?"

"Kind of," Sophie said, and I felt her swallow her pride as she said her next words. "I actually came by to apologize."

"Apologize, huh?" said Derrick meekly. He smiled an empty smile that spread from the corners of his mouth and revealed his teeth. "Whatever for?"

"Well, it's complicated," Sophie replied. "I guess I haven't been very nice to you, Derrick. You've been trying to roll out the welcome mat, and well...I haven't been very kind about it. Selfish old me, I guess."

"Is that right?" He leaned on the doorframe, mirroring her posture. It gave me the strangest feeling that he was some kind of predator, one who tracked and stalked his prey and learned its nature before pouncing. "Well, all is forgiven with me, Sophie. You know that."

Sophie knew all too well how much Derrick forgave. But I tried to put that thought out of my mind as she went on, speaking quickly to seem apologetic, just like we'd practiced.

"Yes, and well, uh, I was wondering if maybe I could come in, and we could talk about things. I know it's late, and you're probably busy, though. Perhaps I should come back tomorrow."

He adjusted the belt of his pants and buttoned his shirt, trying to do it absentmindedly like he wasn't attempting to smarten himself up. "Well, it is late. But I've always got time for my Sophie, don't I?"

"That's great," I said. "That's really terrific."

He stepped back and motioned her in. We watched the door close.

"This is as good a time to remind you as any..." said Trevor, "...that if you leave this car before I go to make the arrest, we cannot legally hold him."

"Thanks for reminding me," I said listlessly.

Suddenly, I could see them again, the shadow of Sophie's back as Derrick led her into the kitchen. He motioned her to sit, and she did so, casually picking the chair by the window. Do you want some coffee?" said Derrick. His voice sounded a little more crackly on the receiver, and Trevor banged on the box.

"Love some," Sophie replied. "It's been a long day. Max Fircress is trying to sue me, wouldn't you know it."

"Is that right?" he said as he filled the greasy kettle from the sink. I tried to imagine what it was like in that kitchen, with the air of fried fat and oil hanging in the air. Derrick moved away from the table by the window, presumably to make the coffee, and was lost to view. "Take your hat off, Sophie," he said. "It's not very often I get to see those lovely locks."

"You creep," I said.

She smiled and laughed. We watched as she removed the hat, put it on the table, and unzipped her coat for good measure.

"He's going to see," I whispered to Trevor.

"He won't," Trevor replied. "She has to take her coat off, or it looks suspicious." Then he shushed me. Sophie was speaking again.

"...says I made an agreement to look after his kid, and now he's suing me for negligence and dereliction of duty. Can you believe it?"

"I don't think you'll have to worry about him, Sophie," said Derrick. "His days are numbered. You know I know his brother?"

"His brother-in-law? Winston Locklow?"

"Yeah, sure. That guy. Pompous ass, but a nice one. Not like Max. Those rich guys are all the same, Sophie. Not that I've got anything against money. But money didn't stop us from having a good time when we were young, did it?"

"I wonder just how well they know each other," Trevor muttered. "He's downplaying it so as not to seem suspicious, but they flew in together a few days ago. You can't fool me, Derrick," he said, and I realized that this was just as personal for Trevor as it was for me.

"Anyway, that Fircress..." said Derrick, then muttered, "...stupid name, anyway. That guy's going down. You know they're saying he faked all of his business stuff? He was selling cheap pine and passing it off as that sustainably forested, eco-friendly horseshit. Can you believe that?"

I raged at that but held my tongue. My lawyers were currently in the process of demonstrating beyond any reasonable doubt that it had been Winston who'd directed the company to use fraudulent business practices, not me.

"Anyway, Winston..." Derrick said, "...would very much like to see Max gone from this place. And once his reputation's destroyed, he and that spoiled brat of his can take a hike. And that's if I don't arrest him first."

"You've always known the difference between what's right and what's wrong, Derrick," Sophie replied. I could practically hear her saying it through clenched teeth. "That's one of the things I always admired you for."

"Well, thanks, Sophie. I appreciate that. Guess it's why I make such a good sheriff." Derrick had filled the cups and set one down in front of Sophie.

"The truth is..." Sophie went on, "...I didn't just come here to apologize, Derrick. I came to tell you that I need your help. Max is threatening to sue, and I don't know how to pay him. I wanted to ask you if you could help me in any way. You must know a lot about the law, being sheriff and all."

"Damn, she's clever," said Trevor.

"Sure," said Derrick while we listened. "I know plenty about that. The question is, Sophie..." he said, scratching his beard, "...should I? I mean, do you deserve that?"

I saw him in the window now, drifting towards her like a shark in the water, before he sat down at the table. We could see them both now, and I had the strangest feeling I was watching a stage play. "After all..." Derrick went on, "...you have been unkind. Not like my Sophie at all. But then, I can't blame ya if Max Fircress has had his hooks in," he said—his laugh, cold and humorless.

I seethed. "You little bastard," I said as if he'd be able to hear me.

"Hush," said Trevor. "Quiet now."

"It's true," said Sophie. "There's no reason for you to help me, Derrick. But I'm here, hat in hand. Asking for forgiveness. Asking for your forgiveness. In my time of need. Can you find it in your heart to help me? I'll understand if not," Sophie said, shifting in her seat.

Derrick paused dramatically and looked out of the window. He'd always looked like he had so many thoughts going on up there. Now, I saw him for what he was. Derrick was greedy and stupid. And that was all he was. He shifted in his seat and leaned towards Sophie, looking important, looking wise.

"The thing is, Sophie, the Lord helps those who help themselves. You know that, don't you?"

"I do, I do," Sophie said and reached toward him. She took his hand, and I flinched out of jealousy and out of fear. "You're so right. Tell me how I can help myself, Derrick."

I could see every sick impulse in him rejoice at the desperation on her face, the tense, nervous energy in her grip. For a moment, nothing came through on the monitor.

He looked at her hand and studied it. "I guess the question is, how far are you willing to go?"

"Now she's got him," said Trevor.

"Oh, far," Sophie said. "I'd do anything. I'd do anything to be rid of that man. Just tell me what I need to do, Derrick."

There was silence, just a faint crackling on the receiver. Then Derrick's voice spoke again. It was low and slow.

"Would you be willing to hurt him?"

I swallowed, sick to my stomach.

"So you were right," I said to Trevor. "He wants me dead."

"I could hurt him," replied Sophie, and I grew cold in my stomach because we'd rehearsed this with her, and I knew what she was going to say next. "After what he's done to me. After what he did to his wife. They say he killed her, you know?"

I forgive you, I thought to myself. I looked through the window at Derrick's face, flush and filled out from whiskey and fast food.

Derrick looked away. "You know, I never did get to the bottom of why that car crashed," he said. "I don't want to spread rumors, but between you and me, I always thought Max killed that woman, orphaned that girl. So did Winston."

You filthy, rotten liar. I was nauseated by him.

"If I..." Sophie said slowly. "If I agreed to...I mean, if I followed your advice. What would I do?"

"All kinds of things," said Derrick, stroking her hand with his thumb. "Let's say Max were to have a little accident. I could help you with that."

"Really?" she said conspiratorially. "You'd...you'd do that for me?"

"Of course I would, Sophie," he purred while holding her hand. "I'd always help out my Sophie, no matter what she did." She held up her right arm straight. It was the signal she'd agreed upon with Trevor. Quietly, I turned, and we nodded at each other. Trevor undid the latch quietly and opened the car door. He got out, and I listened.

"Well, that's amazing, Derrick. I guess I'll be going now."

"Going?" said Derrick, absentmindedly as he looked at her hand. "Going where?"

"Going back to my parents," Sophie said. I looked anxiously at Trevor as he paced towards the door, unholstering his pistol.

"Why don't you stay here?" Derick said. "After all, this is where you belong, don't you think?"

Sophie stood up. "No," she said, dropping the act. "I think I'll be going."

He stood up too. I gasped and looked at Trevor. He was moving slowly up the stairs to the porch now, gun held to the side of his head, in both hands. But Derrick was talking, and his voice had a different quality now, wheedling, whiny, reedy.

"You think you can just show up here, say a thing like that, and leave? That's not right. You're staying right here."

"Oh, no," Sophie said, her arm still held high in the air, her voice almost inaudible through the crackling on the receiver. "I won't."

"What the hell are you holding up your arm for like that? Put it down."

I looked at him. There was silence.

"But I can't, Derrick," said Sophie slowly.

She'd backed out of the window, and all I could see were his piggish little eyes in his swollen face. "Why not?" he said and took a step towards where she was standing, just out of my view.

Please be okay, I prayed.

"Because it's the signal," said Sophie. I saw Trevor had his hand on the doorknob.

"Go in," I said breathlessly to no one. "Go in, Trevor!"

"Signal?" said Derrick. "Signal for what?"

Suddenly he was gone, out of sight too, and I frantically started to get out of the car when his voice bellowed deafeningly on the receiver.

"SIGNAL FOR WHAT?"

There was a moment then, a silent moment, where I was sitting here, watching, powerless in the middle of all the tension. I realized that there was nothing I could do now.

"You bitch," Derrick said on the receiver. "You fucking stupid bitch, do you know—"

But his words were interrupted by a deafening crash as Trevor busted down the door.

"POLICE!" he yelled, and I was shocked at his tone. I heard a thump, probably Sophie, dropping to the floor. "Put your hands on your head!" he said.

Derrick scrambled, running for the back door like Trevor had predicted. But by that time, Trevor had darted through the room and thrown him over the table. There was scuffling, scraping, yelling, and then the sound of somebody gasping for air, breathing hard. I realized it was Sophie and got out of the car.

Chapter 29

Sophie

In a tiny room at the back of the precinct was a stool, a chair, and a table, with a one-way mirror. Max and I stood behind it, watching the pathetic scene unfolding before us.

"Derrick Masters, I've placed you under arrest for conspiracy to commit murder and manslaughter in the first degree," began Trevor for the third time. "You have the right to remain silent, but anything you do say can be used against you in court..." said Trevor before Derrick interrupted him.

"YOU LITTLE CREEP!" he yelled, wincing as he struggled to free himself from the cuffs. "I'm gonna get you! You made that fucking bitch entrap me. You hear me? This is *ENTRAPMENT—*"

"You have the right to an attorney before we question you. You have the right to have an attorney with you when we question you—"

"—I won't need a *damn lawyer!*" Derrick screamed, really screamed, like a child this time. "I need no one. I'm the goddam sheriff of this shitty little island, and I decide who goes to jail. Not you, Trevor, you self-righteous little—"

"If you cannot afford an attorney, one will be provided for you before we question you if you wish..." continued Trevor, "...and if you decide to answer questions now without a lawyer present, you have the right..." he said, wrapping it up in a harsh tone of voice as Derrick carried on screaming, "...to stop answering *at any time*."

"Are you okay?" said Max, turning to me.

"Believe me, Max," I said over Derrick's muffled wailing from behind the screen. "That was practically therapy."

We'd got Derrick to the station an hour ago. Trevor had suggested we let him stew, but it wasn't working. "I have to get him to confess so that we can move forward with Winston," he'd said as we stood in Derrick's old office a few minutes ago.

"How are you going to do that?" I asked. Trevor was looking through the boxes of files and cabinets. Anything that could be used against Derrick. The reports sat in the center of the desk, their pale paper looking ghostly, unpleasant. I could see diagrams on them of wheel axles and the occasional photograph of twisted metal.

Oh God, Max, I'm so sorry, I thought, looking at them. I tried to look at him, but we hadn't made eye contact since he'd found me at the jetty. Now that we were in the same room as each other, neither of us really knew what to say.

"I'm going to apply a little pressure," Trevor had said. "It's the only thing I *can* do at this point."

There in the interrogation room, we waited until Derrick had finally stopped screaming. Now, as Trevor spoke, he was quieter, and authoritative but not fired up. He spoke simply and plainly.

"Listen, Derrick," said Trevor, placing his hands gently on the table and leaning down. Derrick craned his head up slowly. Suddenly, the reality of the situation became clear to him. His posture stiffened, and those dark, shiny eyes seemed to widen in

S.E. Riley

their hollow sockets. He understood now, understood that he was helpless and weak before the power Trevor held over him. I watched his jaw twitch as he looked up at Trevor through the glass. He looked like a frightened rat, ready to run at the first sign of an escape. But as Trevor spoke, his shoulders slumped, and he listened, watching and waiting for a glimmer of hope in the situation which had befallen him.

"We don't want you," said Trevor, relaxing and placing one foot behind the other. "It's Winston we want. I know he put you up to killing Winnie, and I know he helped you falsify the documents."

"You can't prove that," hissed Derrick between gritted teeth.

"Not yet," said Trevor. "But you can help me, Derrick. You can help me prove it. And if you do, there's a solid chance I can speak to the D.A. to reduce your sentence and look favorably on the awful things you've done. You're not all bad, well..." murmured Trevor with a hapless chuckle, "...you're mostly bad, Derrick. In fact, you're one of the most despicable humans I've ever met." Derrick snarled at that. "But you do have one advantage. You're not smart enough to have thought up this on your own, and, what's more, you had nothing to gain from it. If you agree to testify to that...if you tell the judge the truth, and if you tell him what Winston did to Max and Winnie, what Winston wanted you to make Sophie do to Max, well..." Trevor said, turning away, "...exceptions could be made."

Derrick huffed and sat back in his chair, sulking like a child. He stared before him into the dark, blank future that waited for a corrupt, crooked cop inside a jailhouse. "A plea bargain?" he said quietly, looking straight ahead.

"That's for the D.A. to decide," said Trevor. "But tell me, just for old times' sake. What did you have to gain? I can prove you covered up the evidence, and that gives me probable cause,

Derrick. I can certainly prove you covered up Winnie's death and was planning to kill Max. Well, that's enough to send you down for a long time. But what I just don't understand is, why?"

There was silence. Then, Derrick spoke. When he did, it was practically a whimper.

"I needed the money," he said.

"What?" asked Trevor.

"I *said* I needed the *goddam* money!" Derrick said, petulant now. "Okay? We're not all lucky enough to live with mommy and daddy, Trevor. I got bills to pay, don't I? He said he'd help if I...look, they weren't supposed to die. Winnie wasn't...Winston just wanted them injured. He had me plant the tire spikes."

"That's good, Derrick," said Trevor. "Anything you can tell me like that is really good."

"Look," said Derrick. "That was it. That and handling the police on the mainland. Well, that was easy enough to do. But there was always...something else...afterward. Helping him out with that damn land on the other side of the island, helping him with something else."

"Keep talking," said Trevor. "You're doing great."

"Fuck you," spat Derrick, and as I peered at him in the gloom of the interrogation room, I could see there were tears in his eyes. After years of bullying anyone who stood up to him, ruling the roost as sheriff. After all the pain and suffering he'd caused me. Derrick Masters was crying. And as he started to cry, he told Trevor everything while Max and I listened and let it hit us like a tidal wave.

***

Afterward, the three of us sat on the low bit of decking outside the front of the sheriff's office. It was dark, the dead of night, and all that could be heard was the slow roar of the ocean coming from the seafront and the occasional cry of a gull.

"She never told me," said Max, eventually. Trevor and I turned and looked at him. He was practically whispering. I turned to look at him, the man I knew I adored, the man I wanted, broken, devastated by a truth he'd always known.

"All the time, she knew what he was planning, knew he wanted that land," said Max. "And she never told me."

"She wanted to protect you," said Trevor, and then it was my turn.

"She saw the best in him," I said, stunned at myself. "She thought there was a chance of making Winston do the right thing, a chance of making him give up the idea of bulldozing that place. So she hid it from you, hoping he would change, waiting until it was too late."

Who was I to say what Winnie thought, what Winnie had known? I'd never known her. I was just someone who had come along one day, into Max's life, into Mindy's life. But I was speaking, and I hoped it was a small comfort to Max that his wife had done what she'd done out of love for him and Winston. Perhaps I'd earned the right to speak about that since some part of me had feared treading in the ghost of Winnie's footsteps all along, from the moment I saw Max, from the moment I realized, beyond a doubt, that I would always, always feel this way about him.

"When you feel up to it, we can discuss the next step," said Trevor uncertainly, and I looked back at him. This had been a search for right and wrong, but it was clear my brother hadn't understood the personal cost.

"Let's discuss it now," said Max. I turned away from Trevor and looked at him. "Max..." I said uncertainly. Despite everything that had happened to force us apart, I cared for him and felt the darkness of our lives easing a little, just a little, in one another's company. I didn't want to put him through more loss and sadness to do with all of this so soon. But when I saw him there, in the moonlight, I realized that he had given himself up to those strong ideals and principles he had. And there was nothing I could say to dissuade him.

"The next step..." Trevor continued, "...is for you to set up a meeting with Winston. We'll wire you, Max, but I'd like Sophie there as well."

"Why me?" I said nervously.

"If you feel up to it..." said Trevor, "...it'll look good. Right now, the fact that you two know each other, and have a history, isolates Winston. We know he was planning to get you involved in getting Max out of the way. Seeing you on Max's side, well, that'll rattle Winston. We might push him to do something actionable or goad him into saying something for which he's indictable. That's the long and short of it."

I didn't want to do this. God knows walking into Derrick's filthy house and letting him put his hands on me had been enough excitement. I was exhausted, dreading each second that ticked away on the clock. But if it helped Max...

"I'll do it," I said. "If you will, Max."

Max looked at me. Was there something else there, something past the sorrow and the pain in his gorgeous blue eyes which beckoned to me? I was no longer sure.

"Well, that's settled," said Trevor. "I need to go over a few more things before I drive me and Sophie home. Max, go get some rest.

I want you to set up the meeting somewhere public but not too busy. Within 24 hours is ideal. If Winston learns we're charging Derrick, he'll bolt. I can't have that. Understand?"

"Nor can I, Trevor," Max said, looking out at the empty street in front of us. "Go do what you need to do."

Trevor got up and walked inside. I heard the door slam shut behind him. Max and I were alone.

Silence sat between us, uneasy and full of those thousands of hesitations. What must be said and unsaid. What need never be said, and what will always need to be said.

"Is Mindy okay?" I asked. My voice felt small, and I realized I was nervous about being alone with him again.

"She's fine," said Max. "She's with Mrs. Langley now. I've asked her to spend a few nights at Fairview. Doors locked, with extra security measures in place. I'm at one of the hotels in town until this is sorted out."

I nodded, happy to know that Mindy was being looked after.

"She really misses you," said Max.

"I miss her too," I said. "I don't know what I'll do without her."

"You don't have to be without her," said Max, smiling curiously like I'd said the silliest thing in the world. "I would never keep her from you. She told me you're her best friend, you know."

"Is that right?" I said, and I felt my heart flood over for Mindy. I wanted to feel the softness of her hair or hold her hand again.

"Maybe you can come and see her when this is over," said Max.

"I'd really like that," I replied. "I'd like to come and see the both of you."

Max looked at me, and I looked back. He looked so rugged and outdoorsy, there, in one of his plaid shirts, with a pair of thick, tan dust boots which had made a series of imprints in the sandy ground. For a moment, the heaviness and weight of the world seemed to lift off our shoulders, and it was like we were two teenagers, running wild and wanted.

"When this is all over—" said Max, uncertainly.

"We'll talk..." I said peacefully, "...when it's over."

"I would never ask you for anything," said Max. "Only, now I find myself waking up and wondering where you are. I find I'm at a loss. Do you feel that way too, Sophie?"

I looked at him, sighed, smiled, and fought back the tears.

"You..." I said, "...are one of the most wonderful men I've ever known."

"And you..." he replied, "...are the most amazing woman."

I smiled a real smile now, with my teeth showing. He looked back. For a moment, I thought how he must have been before Winnie died—strong, a little less thoughtful, a little less wise. I thought, sadly, that there was nothing I'd want to change about my life now that he had been in it. I would have lived through it all just to have had what I had with Max.

And what was left of it?

We'd find out tomorrow.

Chapter 30

Max

That night, after Trevor had driven Sophie home, I went back to the hotel room I'd rented and slept. I couldn't be at Fairview. Not now, in that silent house, where memories of Winnie walked the floors and every word that came out of my mouth was a lie to Mindy. I stared at the still ceiling fan above me while the first frost of the year crept slowly up the windowpanes and the hours went by.

I knew two things without a doubt now. The first was that Winston was a murderer. He'd killed my wife, Winnie, the mother of my child, for the sake of profit. That feeling sparked nothing but a sick nausea in my stomach which had left me unable to eat, unable to do anything except seek an awful revenge. And the other?

The other was that Sophie still wanted Mindy. She might not want me, but I hadn't doubted the bond between them, which was still as strong as ever. And I knew I'd made the right choice at the notary's office last week.

Eventually, as a gray dawn came into life, and the sounds of cars, motorbikes, and the occasional boat motor began to sound outside my window, I sat up. Sleepless and bleary-eyed, I picked up my phone, opened it, and stared at Winston's name in my contacts. Unthinkingly, I pressed his name.

The rings seemed to last forever. But eventually, the dial tone clicked, and I heard him, that old, familiar whistling high-pitched voice with the Southern drawl, except this time it had a whole new meaning. The man I was speaking to on the phone might be my brother-in-law, but hell if I recognized him.

"Hello, Max," Winston said coolly. No wisecracks or highfalutin greetings, no 'Maxy-boy' now. "What can I do for you on this fine morning?"

His candor, his calm, and politeness chilled me to the bone. Again, I wondered. *Could this man really be my enemy?* But then I remembered what Mindy had told me in the hotel room and shook myself half-mad at the thought. I might not be able to trust anyone, but I could trust her to tell me the truth.

"Hello, Winston," I replied. "I presume your lawyers have heard from mine at this point?"

"I hate to do this, Max," said Winston, and I heard the blocky, scratchy sound of the wind for a moment on the line. He was somewhere high up, hilly, maybe. He was still on Criker's Isle, that was for sure. "I really do. But even if we're disagreeing, let's try to make it a gentleman's disagreement, can't we? After all, we are brothers. By marriage."

"Don't you mention my wife," I said. I couldn't help it. I could hardly contain myself. "Don't mention my marriage or Winnie to me."

There was a silence on the phone. He must have realized then that I knew, that I finally knew. And he'd be checking on Derrick if he knew that. *Damn!* This wasn't part of Trevor's plan! I listened, not knowing what to say to assuage his anxiety.

"As you say, Max," said Winston, as though I'd asked him not to put his feet on the couch. The callousness and coldness of the man appalled me, and made my flesh crawl.

"Sophie and I would like to have a talk with you," I said.

"Oh, Sophie? The nanny? You're making decisions together now, are you?" replied Winston. I could hear a subdued and cruel cackle somewhere in his throat. "I didn't pick you for one who needed the *help* to run his affairs."

"Sophie isn't the *help*," I said. "I'll meet you at Bushey's Diner. Six o'clock tonight. You'll be there?"

"If you think it'll help, Max," said Winston. "I'm not sure I should talk to you without a lawyer."

"Perhaps an arrangement can be reached without our lawyers," I said. "If you come alone."

"Quite happy to, Max," said Winston. "Quite happy to."

He hung up.

My cell fell out of my hands. As I sat on the side of the bed, my breathing was labored, and I felt as if my ribcage might explode. For a while, I sat there, exhausted. I thought about where Sophie was now, what I'd gotten her mixed up in.

When I'd recovered, I called Trevor. He picked up immediately; I could tell he'd been sitting by his phone, waiting for my call.

"Bushey's Diner. Six o'clock," I said.

"Thanks, Max. You and Sophie?"

"Yeah. He's coming alone."

"Take whatever precautions you feel are necessary. Some boys from the mainland are coming over this afternoon. They can equip you both and brief you. Max?"

"Yes?"

"If he's coming alone, I'm positive he will be armed."

***

Darkness lay over Criker's Isle by the time the evening came. Lamps were low, and the beams of the streetlights stretched out over the ground as we drove to the diner.

I'd picked Sophie up on the corner of Main Street. She looked as unslept and tired as I did.

We said nothing on the drive, pulling low, tight to the corners. I've never been anxious about driving—not even after what happened with Winnie three years ago. But tonight, I drove smooth and steady, almost hesitant to turn the corner in each bend of the winding road which led up into the hills.

When the lights of the diner were visible, somewhere in the night, the cry of a coyote or a fox sounded, and the scent of woodsmoke hit my nose as we passed a farmhouse nearby. Someone, somewhere had lit a fire against the cold.

We pulled into the diner. I turned the engine off, and for a moment, we sat in the car.

"Are they watching us now?" asked Sophie.

I nodded.

"Can they hear what we're saying?"

"Of course. We're both wired."

"Okay."

I looked straight into Sophie's green eyes. I saw shoulders my hands had touched, a waist I'd held, legs I'd spread apart and would again without a moment's hesitation. I felt my heart thudding in my chest. I don't know why. Maybe it was because I knew everyone could hear us that I said it. But I said it then, the words I'd felt arriving for months now.

"I love you," I said to her, reaching out and taking her hand. These words had more meaning and depth to them compared to when I said them before.

She clasped it, feeling my warmth. There was a smile and there was pain in her face, and a tear brimmed at the corner of one of her eyes.

"Promise me you'll be safe," she said.

"I promise," I replied.

We got out and walked up to the diner.

Inside it was warm, hot, in fact. As I'd predicted, no one was there at that time on a weekday. All except for one person, of course.

There was something frightening about seeing Winston there, in the diner, with his back turned to us. That black hair perched on his head, coiffed today. That wasn't like him. He wore a suit, a loose-cut, baggy suit, and he hadn't taken off his raincoat or scarf. He was just sitting there in the back of the room.

I took Sophie by the hand, and we walked toward him. He didn't stand up to smile or shake my hand. Instead, he just *sat* there, motionless. When I sat down opposite him, I looked at him.

He looked tired. Haunted, even. There were dark circles around his eyes, and he seemed thinner, paler. Had he been drinking? There was a faint smell of it somewhere, but I wasn't sure. But what was really different about Winston was somewhere else in his face, not in anything I could see, but in how he looked at us. He was empty. The mask had been taken off, and there was nothing but greed and malice behind it.

"What exactly did you call me to this filthy little dive to discuss?" he said.

"We came..." I said, "...to get the truth."

"And to negotiate peace," said Sophie. "Max doesn't want to fight with you—"

He held up a hand. "Quiet, you. I won't have some *nanny* lecturing me."

He turned to me.

"I can't give you the truth, Max. To be frank, I can't even explain why I've done what I've done. Only that I won't ever confess to what I did. Especially not since it's quite clear to me the two of you have been bugged by that delightful little Deputy Sheriff."

Crap! Winston knew we'd be wearing wires, recording information. The metal on my chest felt a thousand times heavier. Sophie let out a gasp too, and I rested my hand on her arm. Whatever happened now, we couldn't show weakness in front of Trevor.

"All I came to tell you, Brother Max..." said Winston slowly, tilting his head to one side, "...is that the sale of the forestry areas on the eastern shore came through in the last 24 hours. You are currently looking at the largest landowner on Criker's Isle. And with land, Max, follows development."

"There's no way anyone is going to let you get away with the things you did," I replied. "There's no way *I* am going to."

"Max, my dear," giggled Winston. "You will be leaving soon enough, I believe."

"Leaving where?" I said, dumbstruck by how amusing he found all this.

Winston looked a little puzzled at that. "Leaving Criker's Isle," he replied. "Of course."

"Max isn't going anywhere," I replied.

"*Au contraire.* Max has nothing here. I do. Max's reputation is in tatters. Mine is not. Max's business is failing. My business, little Sophie, has just begun."

"And what will the people of this town think..." said Sophie, "...when they discover what you did to Winnie?"

"There's no way..." Winston replied, this time with a savage glint in his eye, "...that a trainwreck teen runaway and a broken-down, lazy billionaire can ever, ever prove the ridiculous claim that I harmed my sister. And there is no one..." he continued, smiling, "...who would ever confess to such a thing."

"Only Derrick did," I said casually.

"What?" said Winston.

"Derrick's agreed to testify against you, Winston," continued Sophie. "He told us all about you and what you did. Told us how you paid him to plant the spikes, fake the reports. Make it look like an accident. But you didn't count on one thing."

"What's that?" said Winston, jaw ticking. "*If* any of this tall tale were true?"

"Sophie," I said quietly. "You didn't count on Sophie coming here. And there's something else that doesn't fit in your plan, Winston."

"*WHAT DOESN'T FIT?*" snarled Winston. His hands were stretched out on the table now like he was ready to turn it over and run for the door.

"You thought Derrick might be able to find some way to get to me, hurt me," said Max. "Then you would control things. Fairview would be yours. Criker's Isle would be yours. My business."

Winston didn't say anything, but I paused and could hear him breathing. I could hear the rapid intakes of breath, shallow and hoarse. The guy was starting to panic.

"You didn't count on the fact that it's not going to you," I said. "It's going to Sophie."

"Max?" said Sophie quietly.

"It's been done already. I signed the papers this morning. On my death, Sophie inherits my wealth, property, and business in trust for Mindy. Because she's the person I really trust. And it took finding her to realize that you, Winston..." I said with a certain delight, "...are the worst thing that ever happened to me."

"Max? Is that...Is that true?" Sophie said, and our eyes met.

I nodded. "I needed to know that there would be someone to look after her."

Winston stood up. "I've had just about enough of listening to you two," he said. "I'm going now."

I stood up and reached out a hand. "I wouldn't advise that, Winston."

"Don't tell me what to do!" he yelled, and suddenly there it was, like Trevor said, the flash of metal, the gun coming out of his coat, in both his trembling, boney arms, pointed at us.

"Sophie!" I shouted. "Get behind me!"

Sophie did, and we stared at Winston.

"Winston, you don't want another death on your hands," I said slowly and carefully. It was hard not to laugh. He looked so ill-at-ease with the instrument of death in his hands.

Things had always come so easily into those soft, manicured hands, I thought. *Funny that they were never at home there.*

"Oh, to hell with the both of you," said Winston, and ran.

He ran right out of the door.

Right down the steps.

Right into the light, which shone on him.

Right into the ambush Trevor had set, the officers waiting down there in the dark around the parking lot of the diner, State Troopers and rangers, Trevor and the other deputies, and even the marshal who patrolled the ferry on his off-nights, all there. All with their guns raised at Winston while the white spotlight balanced on a squad car illuminated with the same brilliance as the sun, glowing over the parking lot and dazzling him where he stood at the foot of the stairs.

***

For a long time, I sat, frozen, next to Sophie in that diner. We held each other. Then we kissed. "I didn't tell you," said Sophie between sobs. "I might have died, and I'd never got to tell you."

I looked at her curiously. "What? What, Sophie?"

"I'd have never got to say it," said Sophie, still inconsolable. "Max Fircress..." she continued, "...I love you, as well. I love you so much. I don't know what I'd do without you."

I held her head while we sat there on the floor. "Then I'm the luckiest man in the world," I replied.

And I meant it. But Winston? Winston wasn't so lucky. I suppose despite all the money he and Winnie had been brought up with, he was never as lucky as I was in some ways. He'd bolted at the ambush and fled, down the road from Bushey's Diner, then off the track into the forest. Officers followed on foot, and there were dogs. Not that they needed them. Winston made so much noise, shrieking and cursing at them, that they kept his trail to the end of the creek, which led out, around the slope on the other side of the airfield. Eighteen officers were in pursuit, and it was only a matter of time before they ran him down. Trevor told it to me as gently as he could, but I could see from his face that the scene shook him up pretty good.

Breaking from the treeline, Winston had stood on the sea cliffs. Rather sadly, I thought that he must have known there was no hope for him, as he saw them coming through the trees with their flashlights, dogs, and guns. They had him surrounded by a clump of gorse bushes at the end of a promontory.

Trevor, who had led the chase, told him to surrender now, but Winston, always certain he knew better than everyone else and always sure he was better than this little island and all the little lives upon it, drew his gun, thinking he could break away. He fired three shots but didn't hit a thing. And when the officers returned fire, one of the bullets, though none of them knew whose it was, caught him in the shoulder. Winston, knocked back by the force of the blow, turned to fall but found there was nothing there to catch him, because he was falling now, falling from the cliffs and into the waves of the ocean, too dark to see the waves.

Sophie told me the name of that place, the place where he fell, comes from when sailor's wives would wait there to see their ships come into the harbor. It was a local and historical site, a point of interest. Its name was *Journey's End*.

Chapter 31

Sophie

That morning, after he'd taken Mindy to school, he came into my room. I was looking out at the landscape through my window in my room at Fairview, enjoying my morning to myself, when I felt Max's strong hands around me. I sighed happily and let him wrap himself around me.

"Missed you last night," I said. I'd gone to bed early before Mindy, actually. I was still exhausted, even though it had been a week since everything had calmed down.

Max didn't say anything but instead let his hand glide down, down to the soft flesh above my panties. Gently, he let his hand inside and began to touch me, slowly tracing tiny circles on my clit with his middle finger.

I could practically have swooned, not least because as I rocked my hips back and forth, welcoming his hand, I could feel how hard he was behind me. I gently, coquettishly let my behind brush up against him, feeling his manhood stiffen at the touch of me. Eventually, his hands reached out and freed my panties from my legs, and I turned around to kiss him and give him what we both needed and wanted so badly.

Not that we hadn't been taking advantage of the peace and quiet. Max and I had been tossing and turning in one another's arms as much as we could during the day, only stopping when it was time to fetch Mindy from school. Despite all that had happened, we still couldn't keep our hands off each other. The warmth and friendship we'd shared during those first few perilous weeks on Criker's Isle had changed into a curious, loving warmth in the bedroom, where we each knew the other's move.

Assured that I was open and ready for him between my legs, Max climbed over me, brushing my cheek with the stubble of his beard. He kissed me before he looked up and said, "You're beautiful. Did I ever tell you that?"

I smiled and put a hand on his lips. I didn't want compliments now, nor affirmation, nor permission. I knew exactly what I wanted, and it was the pleasingly large, thick cock that hung erect between Max's legs. I put my hand on it, feeling its weight and shape like a treasured possession. He shuddered with delight at the easy readiness with which I handled him before I began to ease him between my lips and inside me.

Max gasped and smiled, excited by the warmth within me. He wrapped his strong arms around my shoulders and did the rest of the work, sliding into me gently with steady, shallow thrusts. I moaned and smiled with each one, yearning to be closer to him, as though we could fuse ourselves with these illicit daytime meetings.

"I love you," said Max, looking into my eyes. Those serene, blue eyes, how they guarded a jealous and passionate soul! He could be strong and domineering when he needed to be, but now I was putty in his hands, and he knew it. He pressed his lips to mine, and we moved together, my thighs reaching up the sides of his until they were pressed below his buttocks, holding him, directing him with all the force I could muster.

"I love you too, Max," I said, almost unable to make the words form in my mouth among the plethora of sighs and cries. I could feel my heart racing and delight coursing up from between my legs into my chest, closer, closer, my cries rising and rising in time with his delightful shouts of joy and pleasure.

YES! I came for him, and delight showered down around me, all the way from my shoulders to the ends of my toes, while he took me and kissed me, as everything he'd held back exploded, and I felt him reach his peak, coming hard and long, his ejaculation powerful and exhausting. Afterward, we lay together, tired and sweaty, curled up and cuddling among his sheets.

"You are really something," I said, still breathless from the fantastic sex.

"You've never..." Max said, panting, "...ever, got close to disappointing me. But I have to say, that was somehow even better than yesterday."

We were smiling and happy. Despite Winston. Despite Derrick. Despite it all, all the pain of the past that had come over us. We'd earned this tiny island of pleasure back after all that had happened, which made us think it might never come to pass again.

***

We were in the car later, on our way to pick up Mindy before a family supper. My mom had invited Max and Mindy for dinner. Suddenly, Max asked me something.

"Do you think they'll make Trevor sheriff?" he said.

I giggled. My brother, the sheriff. "I don't know," I replied. "According to the local paper this morning, someone else is the bigger hero."

"Oh, you're *joking*," said Max. "I can't believe you read that. I knew I ought to have thrown it out."

"Guess it must have been nice, though, seeing your name back in the paper."

"It has been a while," said Max, smiling as he stroked his chin with one hand on the wheel.

"You look so sexy right now," I said. "I'm going to have to stop Belinda from pawing at you at dinner."

He laughed, then fell quiet. "Sometimes I can't believe it," he said. "What happened. It feels like a dream."

I nodded. "The nightmare's over now, I guess."

"I guess..." he said, "...but there's a lot still to do. I need to find out the extent to which Winston messed with the company. The damage he did is going to take a lot of work to undo. I might need to go off-island for a while."

I looked away. "I understand," I said. "It's okay. I can stay with my parents..."

"Sophie," he said seriously. "You're coming with us. I need you. Mindy needs you."

I looked at him, fairly certain that the man next to me was the love of my life.

When we arrived, the atmosphere in my childhood home was different. I had never experienced such lightness and easy laughter. Mindy kept my parents and Trevor entertained with her wild, imaginative stories, while Belinda and I would occasionally lean into each other to exchange supportive words or a gentle squeeze of reassurance. Every time I locked eyes with Max, my heart swelled with emotion. He was the reason for this.

I finally had my family back.

Life couldn't be better.

***

"There's somewhere we need to stop," said Max. "Isn't that right, Mindy?"

"That's right," said Mindy. "Sophie likes the beach." We'd been inseparable since I'd returned. Whether it was curling up on my lap with her book or sitting next to me at the table while she drew, Mindy was attached to me during the time we had with one another. But it was true. Our favorite place these days *was* the beach. I'd guessed that Mindy would have a lot of pent-up energy she'd suppressed during the years of darkness following her mother's death. But I hadn't anticipated just how much the beautiful little girl sat next to me in the car would love to run around, throwing a ball or spinning circles like an airplane. There was a sensitive, old soul in Mindy, one which had seen too much hardship to ever vanish. But there was also a courageous little girl, a kid, with all the needs of a kid and all the wonderful attributes of a kid, a kid who loved to play, to run. So when we pulled up at the beach, I was surprised when she took her father's hand solemnly, and they stood there together.

"Sophie," said Max, uncertainly and nervously. "We have something to say."

"We love you!" said Mindy.

I smiled and laughed. "I...I love you too, Mindy," I said. "I really do."

"But daddy loves you just as much as I do," she replied. "Don't you, daddy?"

I looked at Max. Suddenly I started to realize what was happening, and my legs began to shake. "What is this?" I said.

"Mindy and I have something important to ask you. We've been practicing, haven't we?" Max said, turning to Mindy. Mindy nodded. I was trembling.

"Well, say it," I said, nervous. That nervousness was old and tired, but whatever they had to say, I needed to hear it more than anything.

"Sophie, you are special to us," Mindy said, as though repeating lines she'd practiced with her father.

"In fact..." said Max, "...you're family to us. I love you, and so does my daughter."

"And we think..." said Mindy, "...that you too love us! I mean..." she said, correcting herself, "...that you love...us...too. In, like, a big way."

I gasped, laughing with joy, nodding my head. "I do, I do."

Max stepped back. I looked at him.

He was getting down on one knee.

"Sophie," said Max.

"If you like..." said Mindy,

"We would like you to become a part of this family."

"I'd like you as my mommy," said Mindy.

I was astonished. My head span, and my heart raced. *They're proposing to me.*

"And I..." said Max, "...would like you to be my wife."

There was a deathly silence.

"If you need time to think about it..." said Mindy, "...that's fine. But please answer quickly because daddy is nervous."

Max and I caught one another's eye. We had to giggle.

After all, we both knew what I was going to say.

"Yes," I replied. "Yes," I said. Yes, and Forever.

Epilogue

Sophie

Eight months later

It was the beginning of summer now on Criker's Isle, though the climate here meant there was a slight, almost imperceptible chill in the air. Flowers were in full bloom, and the nights were short, followed by glorious sunrises that streaked the land in red. Bluebells and foxgloves grew on the meadows, and the bare trees were gone. Their branches had brought green leaves and shaded us from the sun, and they'd flowered recently.

Max and I knew, now. We always thought, but now we knew that we couldn't be apart. And I knew I couldn't be without Mindy.

I could almost see her now, her little head above the rows of chairs in the churchyard.

Somewhere behind the hills was a cliffside above the waves. The waves had long since covered and washed away a body, a body everybody knew would never be found.

Somewhere, on the opposite side of the church, just over a low stone wall, was a grave, and that grave was bedecked with flowers. I knew, because I put them there myself this morning. I came early so no one would see me, not wanting anyone to catch me, not even Max. But anyone who walked by today after the ceremony will see the grave and know that someone lay there under the earth who was very much loved, and that, to me, was worth more than anything I could ever say to her, should I meet her one day. I wondered if I would, sometimes.

But not now. I was not thinking about the dead now or the past. Though the past spoke volumes, and in it were all the things that made now *now*, made the present what it was.

And now, all I had to do was walk forwards.

My dad was beside me, holding my arm. I could see my mother turn towards me, smile, and blush. Even she, Alice Gardner, the wild woman of Criker's Isle, appreciated a show.

And what a show it was.

Max had the meadow littered with flowers, spring blossoms hand-picked from the trees. There was a surprising number of volunteers who wanted to do it for him. He was a hero in the eyes of most people in the town. They were right, of course, but another hero was also standing next to him under an archway covered in white cloth.

Trevor was persuaded *not* to wear his sheriff's jacket to the wedding, although it took some effort to talk him out of it. He was settled on a three-piece suit Max got for him, in blue, of course. As my father and I walked down the aisle between the two rows of chairs, he grinned and punched the man standing next to him on the shoulder, excited as I'd ever seen him.

That man was wearing a suit, too, though it was the first time I'd ever seen him in one. His broad shoulders meant I could pick him out in a crowd of hundreds, but he stood, quite meekly, at the head of the ceremony, under the archway. He looked more handsome than ever, though he always grimaced when he looked in the mirror, spotting the occasional gray hair. "I look old," he had muttered, but then I wrapped my hands around him and kissed his cheek, and he knew he felt new to me every day. He knew he was my husband.

Or would be, in just a few minutes.

I kept walking forward. On the left hand side, on Max's side, were all the people who mattered to him and Mindy. Mrs. Deleaney and Mrs. Langley flanked Max's aunt. They were beaming.

On the opposite side of the archway was my maid of honor. She, too, took some persuading. Belinda was looking straight ahead, with her shoulders back, standing tall. She was smiling, and I knew it was because she wanted to look happy for me, but I knew something else, which was that deep down, she was overjoyed for me. She kissed me on the forehead this morning, to mom's surprise. "You're the light of my life," she had said. I think she really meant it.

I was forward now, past the aisles, and those two and someone else was in front of me. Someone who was perhaps the key to all of this, the reason all this was happening.

She was still a little shorter than she should be at her age and still a little quiet at times. Sometimes she was a tyke, and sometimes she was an angel. Sometimes she told me that she missed her mother, and I felt a pang in my heart because I knew she wasn't talking about me. But sometimes, she told me she loved me and couldn't wait for me to be her mommy. I told her I wanted to be her mommy since the day I met her.

"You taught me to draw," she would tell me sometimes. That was my favorite thing she said, even though it wasn't true. I didn't teach Mindy to do anything. I just helped her see that she *could*.

Mindy was holding a cushion, a red, beautiful satin-brocaded cushion. On it was a pair of rings. One for me and one for him. She was wearing a garland of flowers on her head.

My eyes moved to Max as I came up close. My dad stepped forward and shook his hand. "Take care of her, son," he said. He was gruff but glowing inside, I knew. I'd never seen my dad get emotional about anything, but when Max and I told him we wanted to get married, I swear to you, I saw a tear in his eye.

My Max. I kept saying it to myself when he was not around to make sure.

"My Max." I stood before him and looked up into his eyes. I hoped that as long as I lived, I would get to see those eyes. They made me strong, guided me. The look he gave me answered a question I'd been asking all my life. I knew many things I didn't used to, but one was that I deserved this man, deserved his love and admiration. I deserved him at night when it felt like we transformed together in delight. I deserved him in the day when he was the kind, caring man I knew, my husband, my protector.

"I love you," he whispered again.

"I love you too," I replied.

Every time we said it, it melted away all my cares, all the things I thought about, including the past.

The past would always be the past, would always cloud this place. Winter would come again, and with it, the memory of what happened here, what happened here ten years ago, and what happened before then.

But that won't be in the past. It will be in the future.

I was looking forward to it.

- THE END -

OTHER SERIES' BY THE AUTHOR

Billionaire Daddy Series

Swoon to the irresistible charms of these powerful, rich, and protective lovers. A riveting collection of 5 standalone, fade-to-black, two hour reads.

Mountain Man Daddy Series

Starting afresh in a sleepy mountain town sounds like the perfect plan, but the women in this series didn't expect sparks to fly in their quest to rediscover who they are after a rough patch in life. Their mountain men swooped in with their quiet confidence and powerful presence, proving that they had made the right decision. A heart throbbing collection of 4 standalone, steamy, three hour reads.

Hadsan Cove Series

What do you get when you mix a second chance at love, a cozy beach town, and already established relationships? A heartwarming collection of 4 standalone, steamy, three hour reads. Best part...you'll get to experience each and every couple's milestones as the main characters become secondary characters in the next book.

Printed in Great Britain
by Amazon

33838117R00148